The Pony Whisperer

TEAM CHALLENGE

JANET RISING

sourcebooks
jabberwocky

Copyright © 2010 by Janet Rising
Cover and internal design © 2010 by Sourcebooks, Inc.
Series design by Liz Demeter/Demeter Design
Cover photography © Mark J. Barrett
Cover images © jentry/iStockphoto.com; ivetavai/iStockphoto.com; lugogarcia/
iStockphoto.com; Kwok Chi Chan/123rf.com; Polina Bobrik/123rf.com;
Alexandr Shebanov/123rf.com; Pavel Konovalov/123rf.com

Published by Sourcebooks Jabberwocky, an imprint of Sourcebooks, Inc.
P.O. Box 4410, Naperville, Illinois 60567-4410
(630) 961-3900
Fax: (630) 961-2168
www.jabberwockykids.com

First published in Great Britain in 2009 by Hodder Children's Books.

Library of Congress Cataloging-in-Publication data is on file with the publisher.

Source of Production: Versa Press, East Peoria, Illinois, USA
Date of Production: November 2010
Run Number: 13661

Printed and bound in the United States of America.

VP 10 9 8 7 6 5 4 3 2 1

To my inspirational friend, Pia

CHAPTER 1

"HEY, PIA," HISSED JAMES, sticking his head over Drummer's stable door, "lend us You-know-who for a bit, will you?"

"What's the problem?"

"I need to ask Moth why she's started to drop her hind legs over jumps, taking the poles with her. I bet it's something I'm doing wrong." James added, "It always is."

I handed James the tiny statue of a tiny stone woman sitting sideways on a tiny stone horse that I always, always have hidden safely in my pocket. It's with me whenever I go to the stable yard where I keep Drummer. Moth is stabled next door to Drum, and no one—but no one—except James and me knows the secret of Epona—code name You-Know-Who—and we've both sworn to keep it that way!

"Thanks!" he said, and disappeared to have a talk with his pony. That's right—a bit of a chat. Because even though her nose is missing and she's nearly two-thousand-odd years old, Epona (Are you ready for this?) has the power to let whoever is holding her hear what horses and ponies are saying and be able to talk with them.

I know! When I found the ancient homage to the Celtic and Roman goddess of horses and heard Drummer talking to me, I could hardly believe it either. But because of Epona, and because I hadn't had the sense to keep what I had discovered about the horses and ponies around me to myself, I had been proclaimed the Pony Whisperer, and all hell had broken loose. I'd helped horses and ponies who had problems; I'd upset people by telling them things they didn't want to hear; I'd even been on TV—twice! Since then, I've tried to live it down and escape the public eye because, believe me, being the Pony Whisperer may sound glamorous (I thought so, too, until it all got out of hand), but Epona gets me into the sort of fixes I try to avoid these days.

Avoiding attention has not been one of my most successful ventures.

Of course, with Epona helping James I couldn't carry on the conversation I'd been having with Drummer, but as Katy and Bean chose that moment to lean on Drummer's stable door like idiot twins, it was just as well. As Katy has red hair and is shorter than me, and Bean is nothing like her, they don't look anything like twins, but you get where I'm coming from.

"Pia," announced Katy, shoving her hair off her face and puffing out her cheeks, "you and Drum have got to be on our team, right, Bean?"

"Yeah, yeah, you've sooo got to be," agreed Bean, beaming at me. Her real name was Charlotte Beanie, but everyone called her Bean. With her height (tall), build (slim), and hair color (blond), she was the perfect match for her elegant palomino pony, Tiffany.

I was delighted they wanted to include me, as I still felt very much the new girl at the yard. Everyone else there had known one another forever, and although my Pony Whisperer title had ensured I hadn't stayed out of the limelight, I didn't feel like I was really one of the gang. Drummer had been welcomed with open hooves by his fellow equines—apart from one, whom I'll tell you about...

"We're taking the Sublime Equine Challenge," Katy announced, "and we just need you to complete our team of four."

"Yeah, we need someone to do the wild card," explained Bean. "Tiffany and I are doing the show jumping, and Katy and Bluey are our cross-country entry, of course!"

"I can't wait!" enthused Katy. "It'll be an opportunity to wear my new cross-country colors."

"What color are they?" I teased. Katy has a thing, bordering on obsession, about purple, and her last cross-country shirt and matching skullcap cover would have made a Roman emperor envious. Her new colors were reputed to be even flashier.

When I'd first met Katy, I had been able to tell her—courtesy of Epona—that her chunky blue roan pony Bluey longed to go cross-country jumping. Katy was nervous, but Bluey's talent soon built her confidence. It was one of my pony whispering successes, before things had taken a downward turn.

"Any chance of starting from the beginning?" I asked them. For an answer, Katy shoved the latest *PONY* magazine under

my nose and jabbed her finger on the full-page ad that read:
ARE YOU READY FOR THE SUBLIME EQUINE CHALLENGE?

Yes, I thought, I definitely am. It was the start of summer vacation, and I was looking forward to six weeks of being with Drummer, entering some shows, and going riding, especially with James, as often as I could. Did I mention that James is totally adorable? No? Well, he is. The trouble is, I'm not the only one who thinks so…

Katy shook the magazine impatiently at me. I read on.

The new up-to-the-minute equine-wear specialists Sublime Equine are searching for the top all-around junior riding team in the country. Could that be you? Four riders under the age of sixteen must each compete in their chosen disciplines of Show Jumping, Cross-Country, Dressage, and the Wild Card Event, where anything goes! After regional qualifiers, the finals will be held at the All-American Jumping Course, Brookdale, at the famous U.S. Jumping Derby meeting. All finalists will win a complete riding outfit from the new Sublime Equine Derby range. For full details on how to enter go to www.sublime-equine/brookdale-challenge.com.

"Wow!" I said. "Drummer could do the jumping, I suppose, or—"

"Not so fast!" interrupted Katy, her green eyes flashing. "Bean and Tiff are doing the show jumping—we just told you that, and I'm doing the cross-country—"

"Not that Tiff's great at jumping, actually, but she's not bad," mumbled Bean, interrupting. In the few months Drum and I had been at Laurel Farm stables, I'd discovered that Katy was just like Bluey—positive, bouncy, enthusiastic, and ready for anything. Bean, on the other hand, had her head in the clouds most of the time, which made things interesting. Although, like I said, I'm still the new girl, and I'm just getting to know everyone. It gets super awkward when Catriona turns up because she does nothing to help me feel at home and makes it clear Katy and Bean are her friends. Catriona—let me explain…

"And we thought you and Drummer would be fantastic at the wild card thingy-whatsit," Katy finished.

"Did you?" I replied doubtfully. "What would we have to do?"

"That's just it," said Katy, waving her arms about in her best windmill impression. "Anything you like! Something whacky. Something different. You and Drum will be great!"

I wasn't at all sure about that and could tell Katy was talking this wild card thing up. She was so like Bluey sometimes, all bouncy and glass-half-full. I'd really much rather do the horse ballet—or dressage as the true professionals called it. "Can't we do the dressage?" I asked doubtfully.

"Oh, yeah, if you like," said Bean, pulling her fringe down and staring at it all cross-eyed.

"Dee-Dee's doing it on Dolly Daydream, remember?" Katy sighed in exasperation at Bean before turning back to me. "With Dolly being so well schooled for the show ring, she'll be perfect. And, being a dappled gray, she looks glamorous, too."

I couldn't help thinking it would be pretty amazing to make up a team and get to Brookdale. I'd gone to the famous arena with my old friend Kirsten to watch the Pony Club Championships one year (mainly because spectators got in free!). I had been terribly jealous of the winners in their Brookdale sashes and couldn't imagine how fantastic it would be to compete there. I daydreamed about riding Drummer in the famous arena. What a wow that would be—one of my more fantastic ambitions ticked off! Plus, I'd seen some of the riding outfits the new company Sublime Equine produced, and they were pretty good. Not all stuffy, but modern and snazzy in great colors. I really liked the idea of myself dressed from head to toe in some classy garb I couldn't ordinarily afford. I supposed I could think something up for the wild card event. How hard could it be? Besides, I was tickled pink to be included—it seemed I was becoming one of the gang.

"OK," I said. "Drum and I are up for it!" I expected to hear some comment from Drummer, who was standing behind me tugging at his feed bag, but then I remembered that while James had Epona, Drummer and I were *incommunicado!* It was really peaceful, actually.

"Hurray! We've got a full team. Fantastic!" shouted Katy, punching the air. "We'd better get practicing!"

"What for?" asked Bean, yawning. We both gave her a look, and she gulped. "Oh, yeah, the challenge. Good idea."

Their work done, Katy and Bean pried themselves off my stable door and disappeared, leaving me to carry on grooming Drummer.

Now Drummer, I have to tell you, is so the best pony. He's a bright bay gelding without any white on him whatsoever. I used to think he was cute and cuddly and well, you know, nice, but Epona soon let Drummer put me straight—you'll see what I mean when I get Epona back.

"Here," whispered James, leaning over the door and furtively handing me Epona. "Thanks."

The moment Epona was in my hand I heard someone humming to themselves. It was tuneless and rather horrible, so I tried block it out.

"Was it you?" I asked James.

"Was it me what?" James's dark blond hair flopped over one eye. It's just the right side of being too long.

"You know, causing whatever Moth was doing wrong."

"Oh, yes, of course it was. She says I'm sitting back too early as we land after the jumps, and that makes her drop her hind legs onto the pole. She can't help it. I have to sort myself out as we're going in for this Sublime Equine Challenge thing."

"Are you? Who are you with?" I wished James was on our team, but remembered that we already had four team members.

"Leanne's team," said James. "Leanne is the dressage diva, of course. Cat asked me if I'd do the show jumping—which is why I need to fix my jumping form."

"Who's your fourth team member?" I asked. I felt slight stirrings of annoyance by the fact that James and Cat were on the same team together and the tuneless singing wasn't helping.

"Dunno. Leanne's the team leader. She probably knows tons of people. She's always out competing at dressage shows," James replied, going into Moth's stable and closing the door.

I went back to picking out Drummer's hooves. "Can you whistle?" I asked him.

"What, with these lips? Of course not! Why do you ask?" Drummer replied before resuming the humming.

"Because you can't sing!" I told him.

"Oh, ha, ha!" said Drummer. "And what's all this nonsense about some team you're cooking up? You all just love thinking up new ways to make us ponies work, work, work, don't you?!"

You see what I mean about Drummer? He's not exactly enthusiasm personified.

"I do hours and hours of work every day at school," I told him. "You think you're overworked if you do an hour's ride."

"But then, of course, we do have to carry your huge carcasses around while we do it," Drummer replied, twirling his feed bag around with his nose because he knows it takes me forever to unravel it again.

I continued picking out mud and stones. Drummer continued to hum and sing to himself. Tunelessly. As I worked, I thought about James being on Leanne's team.

Leanne does nothing but dressage on her good-looking dun pony, Mr. Higgins. Poor Mr. H is always covered up with blankets, even in the summer, to keep his coat clean and lying flat, and Leanne, being a bit older than me and one of Catriona's best buddies, is not exactly my best friend. Actually, I think she's pretty stuck-up most of the time. And she's got multiple ear piercings, so when the sun's out, the glare can be blinding. At least she's civil to me, which is more than can be said for Catriona.

I was going to tell you about Catriona, wasn't I?

Cat hates me.

Let's count the ways.

Cat hates me because everyone says I'm a Pony Whisperer, and she insists that I'm lying.

She hates me, James says, because she used to be the one everyone at the yard sought advice from until I rolled up, able to tell it from the horse's mouth, so to speak.

And Cat really likes James.

And I refused to swap stables with her when I first arrived—Drummer's stable is sandwiched between Moth's and Bambi's, and Bambi is Cat's skewbald mare.

I hope you're following this 'cause it's not easy. Anyway, you get the general gist: Cat hates me; Drum's stable is between Bambi's and Moth's; we both like James (but he doesn't know—I'd die if he did!). Oh, and as if that wasn't enough, Drummer really likes Cat's pony, Bambi, and Bambi hates Drum. So now you know. And if anyone out there has ideas on how we can all live happily ever after, I'm all ears!

9

When I'd finished grooming Drummer, I saddled him up, and as I led him out, Bean asked whether she and Tiffany could ride with us. So I said, yes, of course. It seemed I really was starting to be accepted at the yard. The drive led straight to the bridle path, and we soon passed the place where Drummer and I had found Epona, where I first had heard Drummer and his take on life, and my life had changed completely.

When my mom and I had moved to this area, after my mom and dad's marriage broke down, we had known it was rich with history. There had been Roman settlements in the area two thousand years ago (hence Epona!), and as the highest point for miles around, it had been a popular place for buildings through the centuries. Laurel Farm used to belong to the big house, long since gone. And I mean big—I'm talking servants, carriages, and everything.

With Epona in my pocket, I could hear Drummer and Tiffany chatting. Drummer's bright mahogany neck and black mane contrasted strongly against Tiffany's snow-white mane and golden palomino coat as their heads bobbed in unison.

"What's this about some competition—this Brookdale thing?" asked Drum.

"Oh, that!" replied Tiffany. "Sounds worrying. Still, if it wasn't that, it would be something else. Oh, what's that?" Tiffany put in an abrupt stop, waggled her ears, and then walked on again. She's like that, always on the lookout for anything a bit suspicious. On a bad day she goes along like one of those balls stuck by elastic to its own bat; forward-back, forward-back, forward-back. Bean's used to it and just ignores her. They're completely unalike—Tiff's all "Whaaa!" while Bean's so laid-back, she's practically *zzz*-ing all the time.

"Get a grip." Drummer sighed. "It's just an empty bag of chips."

"Oh, so it is. Phew. You never know..."

"Never know what? When chips might turn nasty?" asked Drum. He's not exactly sympathetic to Tiff's nerves.

"You just never know, that's all. If my ancestors hadn't had their wits about them, I wouldn't be here now."

"So what's your role in the Brookdale bologna?"

"What? Oh, that. Er, let me think. Oh, I remember, show jumping. I hope they won't expect me to slide down that derby bank. No, thank you, I don't do heights!" Tiffany sniffed. "What's your specialty?"

"No one's told me yet!" said Drummer.

It didn't sound like the ponies were exactly bursting with enthusiasm. When we got back to the yard, Katy and Dee-Dee were both outside Dolly's stable wearing identical thunderous expressions. Dolly nickered to Drummer when we got near. Dee's beautiful dappled gray show pony has a bit of a thing for Drummer.

"What's up with you two?" asked Bean. "You look like you want to murder someone."

"Yes, well, you will, too, when you hear," said Katy grimly.

"Tell us," I said, jumping off Drummer and running my stirrups up the leathers.

11

"Dee's mom won't let Dee enter Dolly for the dressage."

Bombshell!

"What? Why not?" exploded Bean.

"Oh, well, get this," Dee whined. "She says we've got too many top shows to go to. Says it will ruin Dolly's chances. Says she's hoping we'll qualify for the Horse of the Year Show."

"But—" began Bean.

"No buts!" interrupted Katy, doing an uncanny impersonation of Dee's mom and sticking her hand up, palm toward us. "Subject closed!"

"Jeez, Dee," I said, "can't you do something?"

Dee rolled her eyes. "What do you think? It's all right for you. Your mom isn't horsey. You know how much I hate being dragged off to shows every weekend. I'd rather be having fun with all of you. My mom's made it clear that while she's paying the bills, she'll have the last say. I never get to have any fun on Dolly. I just wish she was an ordinary pony, like all of yours."

"Excuse me?" cried Katy, her hackles rising.

"Oh, you know what I mean!" moaned Dee, lost in self-pity.

I sucked in my cheeks. Dee's mom Sophie is a showing fanatic and used to getting her own way. She has her own show horse, a liver chestnut called Lester (with some fancy-shmancy show name) and their horse trailer is probably bigger than the house I live in with my mom. And Sophie is the sort of horsey woman who won't take no for an answer.

Pooh! I was getting super excited about this competition. Now we seemed to have failed before we'd even begun.

"You're reprieved then," I heard Drummer say to Dolly.

"Yes." Dolly sighed. "And I was so looking forward to spending more time with you, handsome," she added, batting her eyelashes at my bay pony.

I told you, didn't I?

"Maybe we'll all get out of it." Tiffany sounded hopeful.

"Bet we're not that lucky!" Drummer groaned.

"But what about me? What am I supposed to do all summer?" moaned Dee, picking flaking green paint off Dolly's door with her fingernail.

"Don't worry about that," Katy said brightly, smiling at Dee. "When you're not qualifying for HOYS you can be the team groom."

"Oh, big deal!" exclaimed Dee, flicking her brown hair and storming off in a huff to the barn.

"How about James?" Katy suggested. "He might be on our team."

"Cat and Leanne have already bagged him," I said.

"We have to find someone," Bean wailed, jumping off Tiffany. Tiff woke up with a start, suddenly alert to any tigers or crocodiles or wolf packs that could be lurking—like they do around a stable yard.

"We will!" I said grimly. "We just have to!"

CHAPTER 2

DESPITE OUR DEPLETED TEAM, we began to practice for the Sublime Equine Challenge. At least, Katy and Bean did. I just sat about wondering what on earth Drummer and I could do for the wild card event. What would the judges be expecting? I couldn't get my head around it—whatever could we do that was different and exciting? I couldn't let Katy and Bean down.

I explained the concept to Drummer.

"Why can't we just do the show jumping?" he said.

"Because Bean and Tiff have claimed it."

"Well, ask if we can do the cross-country. I can do that—if I have to."

"Bluey's doing it. He'll die of disappointment if anyone else does it, and he's way, way better at it than anyone else."

"Well, I could just about manage the dressage, I suppose," said Drum in his best martyr voice.

Of course! Now Dee was out, perhaps Drum and I could grab the dressage slot. I thought hard. Dressage isn't our best thing, really. To be honest, we're not great at anything in particular, but we are sort of passable at everything—you know, we get by and win the odd ribbon. We'd probably do a better dressage test than a pathetic wild card routine, I thought.

I found Bean in the outdoor school, putting Tiffany over a few jumps. Katy was doing the groom bit—charging around and changing the height of the poles. She was a bit red in the face, which clashed with her red hair. The effect was sort of a raspberry topped with grated carrot. I didn't think she'd thank me for telling her, so I kept it to myself.

"Me and Drum really want to do the dressage!" I shouted from the gate. I decided it would be better to be positive about the dressage, rather than negative about the wild card event. To be honest, I didn't like my chances much in either. Katy stopped in mid-stride and frowned.

"Oh, OK. We just need a wild card person now," she said. "Hey, Bean, you almost ran me over!"

"Well, you're in the way!" wailed Bean, hurtling toward the next jump, her long blond braid flying out behind her like a tail. I couldn't help noticing Tiffany's peculiar jumping style: between jumps she cantered around all collected, looking every inch the show jumper. Then, three strides away from the jump, she stuck her head in the air, launched herself forward like a rocket, and took off almost straight up, like a Harrier Jump Jet. Upon landing again, she resumed her rocking horse canter and melt-in-the-mouth expression. Weird!

I could hear her muttering to herself as she did it: "Oh, there's the jump…OK…here we go…it's a big one…*I can do it!* Oh, no, I can't…maybe…yikes…*Yes!!!*"

"How do you stay on when she does that?" I asked.

"Does what?" asked Bean airily, as Tiffany did her

15

rocket-launcher-jump-jet impersonation over the planks with a grunt. I supposed Bean was used to it.

I went and told Drummer the good news. He was dozing with his head in the far corner of his stable.

"So we're doing the tip-tuppy thing now?" he said, not bothering to turn around.

"If the tip-tuppy thing is Drummer-speak for dressage, then yes," I told him.

"Oh, good, I can sleep through that," he said, yawning. "I don't suppose…"

"What?"

"There's an eating category? I'm sure to win that."

"You're right there, fatso!" I told him. "In fact, I think I need to cut down your grazing hours. I may keep you in at nights for a while until the grass dies down a bit."

"*What?*" yelled Drummer, swinging around to face me. "Are you *joking?* I hardly eat anything. I barely manage to scrounge enough out there in the field at night by the time Tiffany and that pig Henry have lawn-mowered their way around. It's a wonder I've not been reported to the authorities, I'm so starved."

Henry is a hefty, bad-tempered Dales pony who belongs to an ancient old lady called Mrs. Bradley. I didn't doubt he was a bit of a pig, but Tiffany never carries any weight—she and Bean are both identical in the skinny department. I decided to move the conversation on.

"We need a final team member, so put your thinking cap on."

"James and Moth," said Drummer.

"Oh, why didn't I think of that?" I said sarcastically. "Oh, wait a minute, I know—because he's been commandeered by Cat and Leanne!"

"Pippin?" Drum asked, doubtfully. I gave him a look. Pippin is tiny, and his rider, Bethany, is just a kid.

"In that case"—Drum sighed—"I can't think of anyone. Can Bluey do two events? He's always got energy to spare. He makes me tired just looking at him. Speaking of which, you've interrupted my nap."

Drum is so irritating at times! I decided to turn him out in the field and go home.

When I told my mom about the Sublime Equine Challenge, she thought it was a great idea.

"Oooh, imagine if you qualify for the finals," she enthused, her blond hair bobbing in excitement, "and you get to ride at Brookdale. How thrilling would that be?"

"Well, unless we find our fourth team member, that's never going to happen," I replied. We were munching our way through Indian takeout, plates on our laps, watching TV. Empty cartons littered the side table.

"I've got a new date tomorrow," announced Mom. My heart sank. We moved here to this cottage when my mom and dad split up. Dad went off with some size double-zero chick from work, and Mom kinda fell apart. But since we've been here she's brightened up and she's been looking for love, as they say.

On the Internet.

I know, I know, it freaks me out, but what can I do? She's really careful and sensible about it, and I've promised to support her. Her friend Carol supports her, too, which isn't surprising, seeing as how Carol dates men like we're all on a downward slide toward the end of the world. I blame Carol and her interfering ways for getting Mom into it all.

"That's nice," I said, managing to make it sound as though I meant it. I'm getting better at that. "Who's this one? Old or new?"

"Second date," mumbled Mom, stuffing half a samosa in her mouth and leaving filo pastry crumbs on the side of her face.

"Well, if you're going for Indian food, don't do that," I advised. "It's most unattractive. Who's this guy?"

"His name's Greg. He's a teacher. Divorced. He's got two sons, seven and twelve years old. They live with their mother. He's very nice, and he was very attentive on our first date—and very interested to learn about your passion for horses. Apparently, he used to ride in his youth."

"Oh, good, perhaps he can come and be our fourth team member," I suggested, glumly. "Do you think he can possibly pass as under sixteen?"

"Doubtful—he's got a beard."

"Oh, yuck!"

I was getting fed up with trying to think of someone to complete our team. It was so frustrating! If only my old friend Kirsten didn't live so far away, she'd have thought up something great for the wild card event.

The next day, I was tacking Drummer up to go for a ride by ourselves when James turned up.

"Going riding?" he said.

I nodded.

"Want some company?" he asked. "I'm a bit fed up at the moment."

Naturally, I didn't say no.

It didn't take him long to get Moth in from the field and tacked up, and we rode out along the bridle path that led down to the lake. Moth's bright chestnut coat gleamed in the sunlight, her four white legs moving in step with Drum's black ones. Moth has a white face, too, but you can't see that very well when you're riding next to her, and she always goes along in a hurry, puffing and slamming her hooves down like an old-fashioned charger, with James playing the role of her knight. At least, that's how I see it.

"How's the jumping going?" I asked James. "Did your chat with Moth help?"

"Yes, it did, but it's all been for nothing," James groaned.

"Why?"

"Cat told me yesterday that I can't be on her team. It appears that Leanne had already asked two of her much-more-talented-than-me friends to do the show jumping and the cross-country."

"What?" I cried, my heart leaping.

"Yeah, I know. What a bummer, huh?" continued James. "I mean, talk about a letdown. She's nabbed India Hammond for the show jumping, so I get ditched. Leanne thinks she stands a better chance with India and her amaz-ing pony, the Dweeb, than Moth and me. How rude!"

"But that's wonderful!" I shrieked, sitting up and reining in Drummer. I blessed India, whoever she was—selfish of me, but you know.

"Ow!" said Drummer. "Tone it down, will you? Some of us have big ears."

"Oh, thanks a lot!" James exclaimed, turning in the saddle to frown at me.

"We're looking for someone to be on *our* team!" I shouted, bouncing up and down on Drum.

"Hey, I'm not a trampoline. Sit still up there or get off!" grumbled Drum.

"But…but…you've got four people already," James said.

"Not anymore! Dee's mom's forbidden her to do it—says it'll ruin Dolly's chances of qualifying for HOYS."

"Oh, awesome!" James said, beaming from ear to ear before forcing his face into looking seriously sad. "Bad luck about poor Dee-Dee, though."

"Of course."

"Yeah, of course."

I don't think either of us really meant it. Dee's a bit of a whiner. Well, actually, she never stops whining. I suppose it's hard for her with her mom always at the stables and on her case the whole time, but even so, it's a bit wearing.

We rode on with James in a much-improved mood.

"Got our fourth team member?" said Drum.

"Yup!" I told him, patting his neck.

"So we're still doing it?"

"Yup!"

Drummer sighed. Moth said nothing. She's not very talkative due to her (understandable) mistrust of humans. She was mistreated before James got her, and she'll only talk to James. Of course, he can only hear her when he has Epona. We've tried holding Epona between us so we can both hear the ponies, but it seems she only works for one person at a time.

"What's Drummer's problem?" James asked, hearing me talking to him. James has known about Epona ever since he got hold of her by mistake, but he'd never tell anyone else. I mean, imagine the fuss—everyone would want Epona, and I'd probably have to give her up, and Drummer says that ponies everywhere wouldn't thank us. So that's why we keep her to ourselves.

"Oh, nothing important," I told him. "Let's canter— I'll race you!"

Katy and Bean were ecstatic when we told them.

"Fantastic!" Katy screamed, throwing her purple dandy brush in the air. Unfortunately, it landed on the roof with a bang, which made Tiffany, who'd been dozing in her stable next door, almost fall over.

"But wait a minute..." started Bean. "Who's going to do which event?"

We all looked at Bean. I don't think anyone could believe she had beaten us all to highlighting the problem.

"What?" she said. "It's an obvious question!"

"Well," I said, "we need someone to do the wild card." I really didn't want to get stuck with that again—I'd only just wriggled out of it.

"Umm, I don't think so!" said James firmly.

"Well, what then?" said Katy, her hands on her hips. "I mean, I really, really want to do the cross-country."

We all agreed that Bluey was the best pony for the job.

"Moth can only do gymkhana and jumping," James said.

"But I'm doing the show jumping!" wailed Bean. "I've been practicing!"

"So have I," James said. Moth only ever storms around with her nose on her chest, snorting like a dragon. She clearly couldn't do the dressage—she'd be useless at it. She had to do the show jumping.

"But Tiff's really well schooled, isn't she, Bean?" said Katy, determined to win Bean around. "She could do the dressage—Moth can't."

"I suppose so," Bean agreed reluctantly, biting her lip. "But I'm horrible at remembering dressage test movements. The last time I tried it, I totally forgot the way. It was awful."

I could easily imagine Bean forgetting a dressage test.

"Oh, you'll be fine!" James said breezily.

"But I'm doing the dressage!" I told them. I didn't like where this was going.

"You're welcome to it!" shrugged Bean. "I'll be just as useless at the wild card as I will be at dressage!"

"You'll be fine!" repeated James. "It's settled!"

"I didn't know it was up to you—you've swiped the show jumping, and I've been practicing. Dressage isn't my thing—it really isn't!"

"Stop being so bossy, James," said Katy firmly. "You've only been in the team five minutes and you're taking charge. It's our team, not yours!"

"I don't know why you're making such a fuss," began James, oblivious to Bean's feelings. I didn't understand why I couldn't do the awful dressage—I wanted to, for goodness sake, which is what I told everyone.

"But we need you to do the wild card event," insisted Katy.

"Why?" I said.

"Yes, why?" wailed Bean. "Tiff and I can do it. I'd rather do that than the dressage. Believe me, you really don't want me doing the dressage."

"Pia has a huge advantage—she can talk to Drum and get him to do things none of us could do with our ponies. Don't you see?" said Katy, getting all earnest in an obvious attempt to win us over. "Pia is the natural choice for the wild card—she has to do it!"

There was silence. That I might be a natural choice was news to everyone, but we could see how Katy was thinking. The image of Drum and me doing the dressage faded away. It seemed Bean and I were both stuck with our respective events, however much we didn't want them.

I frowned. "What do you mean, Katy? Explain."

"You just have to think something up. Some sort of routine you can talk Drummer through, something that

23

doesn't rely on riding or tack. You could, er, well, you could…Oh, I don't know, how about something without any tack on at all? Wouldn't that wow the judges? You'd win by a landslide!"

"Yes, Pia!" exclaimed James. "That would be so cool!"

I wasn't convinced. "Wouldn't that be cheating?"

"Why?" asked James, totally getting onboard with the idea. "You need to use the skills you have. Not everyone knows you're a Pony Whisperer."

"It sounds like cheating to me."

"No, you're just pressing home your natural advantage," Katy continued. "Just as Leanne is really good at dressage—she's not going to do the jumping because she thinks she has an unfair advantage in the dressage event, is she?"

When it was put like that, it sort of made sense.

"Does that mean I'm stuck with the dressage?" mumbled Bean.

We all looked at her in sympathy. Katy put her arm around Bean's shoulders.

"You and Tiff can do it! Tiffany does really well, I don't know why you don't enter for more dressage competitions. You'll be great at it."

"Because I can't remember the tests!" Bean said through gritted teeth.

"One of us can call for you," said James. "You can have someone call out the movements if you want to."

"Yes, that would work!" said Katy, squeezing Bean's shoulders.

"That's worse," said Bean, shaking her head. "It confuses me even more." She gave a big sigh. "I suppose I can give it a try," she said. "For the team."

"We'll help you learn your test," I said, impressed by Bean's attitude. I could see her being great at dressage—Katy was right, Tiffany was well schooled, and Bean rode really well. I was, however, really annoyed about being forced into the wild card thing. My attitude sucked.

"Atta girl!" James grinned at Bean.

"You're a star!" said Katy. "Besides, only the three highest scores count, so stop worrying."

"Is that supposed to make me feel better?" said Bean, getting indignant. "I'm just there to make up the numbers, am I?"

"I just thought it would take the pressure off a bit," said Katy, going red. Bean just sighed.

It was settled.

I couldn't help thinking how great it was to be on the team. Shame my event was a pile of poo!

CHAPTER 3

"S o you're on Katy's team now?" I heard Catriona's voice. She and James were outside Moth's stable.

"That's right," I heard James reply good-naturedly. "And we're going to beat your team into the ground, so don't get your hopes up!"

Catriona laughed and told James he had no chance.

I walked over to get Drummer's halter, which was hanging on his door. I always dread seeing Cat. She never misses an opportunity to poke fun at me. I hate the way I feel intimidated just by her being there.

"Oh, there you are, Pia, we were just talking about you!" she smirked. Like I couldn't hear! I pulled my mouth into a fixed smile. Catriona is annoyingly pretty, with short dark hair and elfin features. The other annoying thing is that she really likes James, and as James hangs around with one of Cat's three brothers, I can't help feeling she has the advantage over me. Sooo annoying!

I took myself off to bring Drummer in from the field. He was hanging around the gate, waiting for me.

"Come on, hand over that carrot!" he hissed, edging his way carefully around Cat's skewbald mare Bambi. Bambi put her ears back and snaked her head at him. She can't stand Drummer, and he, for some unknown reason, is totally into her.

I thought about Catriona. I bet she was furious that James was on our team—having him in hers had been a definite coup. I grinned to myself. Too bad, I told myself, Leanne didn't want him so that's your loss.

I still hadn't thought of a thing to do for our wild card routine. I'd gone onto the Sublime Equine Challenge website and printed out the rules and regs. It was pretty complicated. Apparently, to qualify for the Brookdale final each team had to finish in one of the first three places of a qualifier. Twice. And to make it more interesting, teams weren't allowed to enter more than three qualifiers. Tricky. And Katy was right, the highest three scores from each team counted toward the final score, with the lowest score being dropped from the total. Then I had searched for information on the wild card event. The judges will be looking for a performance from an individual that demonstrates a unique partnership with, and understanding of, their pony, it said.

It didn't say whether I had to ride or whether I could be on foot. It did say each show was not to exceed a four-minute duration. It didn't inspire me. No light bulb moment occurred; no mother of an idea popped into my head.

I took Drummer for a ride to see whether I could get my head around it. Drummer took advantage of my lack of concentration and bucked a few times, landing me on his neck.

"You're so not funny!" I told him.

"Oh, but I so am!" he smirked.

We turned into the woods where it was cool and damp. Through the trees I could see the sun sparkling on the lake and Drummer's hoofbeats became silent on the carpet of pine needles. I'd never been in this part of the woods before, but I knew I couldn't get lost if I kept the lake in sight. I was still exploring the countryside near the stables, and finding new paths every time we went riding.

Suddenly, all thoughts of the wild card disappeared as Drummer slammed on the brakes and snorted, lifting his head and holding himself stiffly to attention.

"What is it?" I whispered, my hand on his neck.

"Don't know," he said. "But the ground around here feels a bit funny."

"Funny?"

"Yes. I can't explain it. There's something strange over there behind the bushes. The whole area's giving me the creeps."

I felt the hairs on the back of my neck stand up, and my imagination ran riot. "Should we be getting out of here?" I whispered.

"What? No, no, it's old vibes I'm picking up. Let's take a look," Drum said, walking forward again. I didn't know whether I wanted to take a look. What old vibes? What if they were dead body sort of old vibes. And how old? It was uncanny how Drum could feel stuff.

It wasn't a dead body. We pushed our way through the bushes and there was what looked like a grassy mound with a door in it. A very old, arched wooden door, with rusty nails and a rusty handle. It couldn't be a house, unless the house was either very small or underground.

"What is that?" I said.

"You're asking me?" said Drummer. "Get off and take a closer look."

I slipped out of Drummer's saddle. "Hey," I told him, "no running off and leaving me here. Promise!"

"OK, OK. You spoil all my fun."

I tried the door, but I couldn't make it budge. It was old and mossy and the handle was riddled with rust. Secretly, I was really glad. I mounted Drum again.

"You are so feeble." He yawned.

"Yeah, well, I'd like to see you do any better with your hooves!" I told him, turning for home.

When we got back to the yard, Catriona had gone riding with Leanne, but luckily, James was still around.

"I've just found something very strange in the woods by the lake—" I began.

James held up his hand to stop me. "Grassy hill with a door in it? Looks like a hobbit house?"

"Yes!" I cried. "That's exactly what it looks like. It's not a hobbit house, is it?"

"No, it's an old icehouse," James replied. "When the big house was here, centuries ago, the people stored ice from the lake in the winter to use in the summer. Built into the ground it stayed cold, and the ice stayed frozen for months."

"Wow! I couldn't open the door."

"Oh, I've been in it. It falls away to a huge, dark hole, and you can't see the bottom of it. It's kinda cool."

It didn't sound cool. I was glad the door hadn't yielded.

"How come you know about it?"

"Most of us do—but I think we're the only ones, being as we ride around there. No one seems to care about it. If the city knew it was there I expect they'd think it was dangerous and probably board it up or fill it in."

"Are there any other strange and ancient buildings or things around here I should know about?" I asked him. I was intrigued by the icehouse. It was really spooky. I imagined servants cutting blocks of ice from the frozen lake, loading it onto wagons, and packing it into the icehouse. How cool was that? Oh, actually, that's pretty funny. I'll have to remember that one.

"Oh, probably," said James. "This yard was the farmyard for the same house. The work horses would have been stabled here. The riding and carriage horses would have lived at the coach house."

"Oh, where's that? Can you show me?" I thought an old coach house sounded wonderful. I loved the way the surrounding countryside held such historic secrets.

"No. It's gone. No one can see it. The land"—James paused dramatically—"has reclaimed it."

I had other matters of concern.

"I can't imagine what I can do for this wild card event," I moaned. James threw Moth's old water away on the grass behind her stable and sat on the upturned bucket.

"Well, let's think of something. What can you do that no one else can?"

"Nothing," I replied, miserably, flopping down next to him. "I'm hopeless at thinking things up."

"So do you have any ideas? I can't think of anything!"

"Well…something did occur to me. You could do something like the dog people do," mused James.

"What—agility? I can't see Drummer galloping through a cloth tunnel or weaving in and out of poles."

"No, not agility. What do they call it? Doggie dancing. You know, they put a routine together with music. You and Drum could do that. It would be different."

I thought hard. I'd seen people dancing with their dogs on the television. It looked fun. I could make us both costumes. We could have music. I'd always imagined myself in showbiz.

"That might work…" I began. "But I'd need a theme and music." I felt excited and my spirits lifted a bit. But then they plummeted again: I'd forgotten one thing. The most important thing. I was going to have to sell it to Drummer. I decided I'd defer that until I'd got a bit further with the routine idea. No need to get him into negative mode just yet. I'd wait until I had it all planned out in my head.

The next day, at breakfast, I had to suffer the account of Mom's date with the latest man in her life.

"What a nice man!" Mom said, struggling to open a carton of orange juice. I took a deep breath—I'd heard that before. Most of Mom's dates start off that way. By the fourth or fifth date, they begin to show their true colors and words like nice are replaced with *weirdo, letch,* and *creep.* I always looked forward to the novelty wearing off.

"He was charming and very funny. I think you're going to like him, Pia."

"It sounds as though you do," I said, digging into some toast and jam. "Mom, can I talk to you about this Sublime Equine Challenge?"

"Of course. I was telling Greg about that last night…"

"I've decided to do a dance-type routine with Drummer, you know, like they do with the dogs at Westminster."

"That sounds tricky. Are you sure you can do that?"

"Yes, I'm certain—I can talk Drummer through it (Mom knows I can talk with horses, but she doesn't know how). But anyway, the thing is, I'm going to need an outfit—and so is Drum. Do you think you can help me?"

"I'll try. I used to make your outfits for school plays, do you remember? You looked lovely in that angel's outfit I made for the nativity."

Uh-oh, nativity flashback! I'd been about six, there had been about fifteen angels, and Zoe Braithwaite was the most glamorous with huge, sparkly wings like a fairy queen. Mine were made out of wire coat hangers, and my dress had been an old nightdress. I wondered whether asking Mom for help in the wardrobe department was a good idea. It was too late to backtrack now.

"What are you going to be?" asked Mom. "I've got lots

of old curtains in the attic from our old house, so if you can think up costumes with a floral theme, that would be handy. Did you see the rose Greg bought me at dinner? He's very romantic."

I couldn't stop my head from filling up with images of Zoe Braithwaite. She had looked so glamorous. By comparison, I had looked like a clown, a jester to her queen. A jester…maybe there was some mileage in that idea. Maybe…

"What do you think about Drummer and me being a jester and a queen?" I mumbled, still working the idea around in my head. Drum could wear bells, I could get dressed up like a medieval queen, all flowing wimple and long dress. It might work…

"Or you could both be jesters," added Mom. "Greg's funny, too, amazing sense of humor…"

"Mmmm, we could." My toast had gone cold and so had my enthusiasm for Greg. He sounded like a creep to me. "I need to think about this," I told Mom. Grabbing my bag and Epona, of course, I biked to the yard with the queen and jester idea whirling around my head. It could work. Frankly, I thought, it had to work because time was ticking on, and I had only a week to figure out a routine and get our outfits made before the first local qualifier.

James and Katy thought it was a great idea.

"Great!" enthused Katy.

"I can just see you in medieval outfits!" said James. "Bells are a genius idea."

"I don't get it," said Bean. "What exactly are you going to do?"

"Well, I'm not completely sure yet," I told her. "It's just an idea. It needs work."

"We'll help you work out a routine," offered Katy. "It'll be easy! Drummer will look so cute in a jester outfit with bells on—he'll love it!"

Mmmm, I thought to myself with a sinking heart. I still hadn't told Drummer—and loving it wasn't exactly how I imagined he would feel.

CHAPTER 4

"LET ME GET THIS straight," Drummer said. "You expect me to do that ridiculous dance routine thing we practiced—with bells on—in front of all these ponies? Dream on!"

We had arrived at South Bassett Farm, where the first of the local qualifiers for the Sublime Equine Challenge was being held. James, Katy, Bean, and I had all ridden over—it had only taken an hour but had seemed a lot longer because Bean was trying to remember her dressage test, and we were fed up with hearing it—and now that we'd arrived we were feeling less than confident. South Bassett Farm was where the local riding club held its shows and events. They had a cross-country course in the adjoining woods, and the Sublime Equine team had moved in with all the paraphernalia needed to put on a show.

"Oh, my," breathed Bean, "look at that group!" We followed her gaze to a team of four matching chestnut ponies. Their riders were all decked out in identical riding clothes with blue shirts and pale ties, and the ponies all wore blue and pale blue brow bands. Their blue saddlecloths had the words TEAM DIAMOND emblazoned across them.

"Whoa!" exclaimed James.

"Oh, I wish we'd thought of that!" cried Katy. "My mom would have made us some saddlecloths. We'll have to have some for the next qualifier."

"We'll have to choose a name, first," I pointed out. I didn't like the look of this—there were tons of teams and they all looked much more polished and confident than us. I spotted Bambi and Mr. Higgins tied to Leanne's trailer; Cat and Leanne were grooming them. Their matching red polo shirts had TEAM SLIC on the back of them.

"Team names seem to be the thing," I said, wondering what SLIC stood for, and whether they'd forgotten to add the *K* at the end. Or maybe the letters were too big, and they'd run out of space. "We totally need to think up a name for our team. We're just a number at the moment."

"How about Team Tremendous!" suggested James.

"Or Team Bossy Boy," mumbled Bean.

"Oh, good idea, Bean—you could all be James's Angels, like Charlie's!" James laughed.

"Is that supposed to be funny?" I said.

"Where's the cross-country course?" Bluey said, chomping at the bit. "I can't wait to get going!"

Tiffany looked around the showground. "Is that a paper bag or something worse? What's that droning noise? I hope no one pops a balloon, and I hope my test is soon so I get it over with," I heard her muttering.

Moth kept her thoughts to herself as usual, and Drummer was sulking. Which was better than going on and *on* about how much he didn't want to do the wild card.

Breaking it to him hadn't been as bad as I'd imagined—until I'd mentioned my idea for outfits.

"You expect me to wear some fancy getup?" he'd asked, his ears twitching backward and forward.

"Yes, well, the routine depends heavily on the visual aspect," I'd explained.

"With bells, you say?" More ear twitching.

"Well, yes. Jesters wore bells."

"And you're *not* wearing bells, have I got that part right?" He'd stared at me.

"Mmmm, yes. You see, I'm the queen. A jester entertains the queen. He makes her laugh."

"I'm a figure of fun? A clown? You're glamorous, and I'm the stupid one?" Ballistic ear action.

"It's only for four minutes," I'd mumbled, aware that Drummer wasn't buying into it.

"Four minutes..." he'd mused. "What's in it for me?"

"Excuse me?"

"What do I get out of it? What's my motivation?"

"Er...well...you get the satisfaction of doing your part for the team. It's a team effort, and you'll be supporting Moth and Bluey and Tiffany." I had felt pretty pleased at thinking that up.

"OK, I get all that," Drum had said dismissively, "but I'm talking about me. What do I get if I do this...this... pointless fancy costume parade? With bells."

"What do you want?"

"To stay out at night. No more talk of me staying in and going on a diet."

I had thought long and hard. The grass was going off a bit now so it would probably be all right.

"Deal!"

But when I'd tried his outfit on him, Drummer had protested all over again.

"What's this stupid hat thing?" he'd said when I'd put the ear caps on him. They were knitted ear protectors, worn by show jumpers to keep out noise and flies. I'd managed to find some red ones at the tack shop, and Mom had sewn on some yellow diamonds. We'd decided that Drum's bay coat would look good in a red and yellow jester outfit, with a diamond pattern and bells sewn in strategic places. I'd bandaged each of Drummer's legs—two red bandages, two yellow—weaved some red and yellow ribbons in Drummers mane and tail, and decorated a yellow halter with tiny red felt diamonds. With little jingling bells from the pet shop sewn onto the tips of the ear protectors and each leg bandage, Drum *ting-a-ling*-ed whenever he moved. I had been very proud of my efforts, and thought Drum looked the part without going over the top.

Drum hadn't agreed.

"So what are you going to wear?" he'd asked me, shaking his head. The bells had given a satisfactory *ting-a-ling*.

"I've got a wimple…"

"A what?"

"It's a pointy hat with a chiffon scarf tied at the top…"

"Like a witch?"

"I suppose." I had sighed, worn out by Drum's negativity. "And a floaty yellow dress thing to wear over my jodhpurs. It's really you they'll be looking at."

"Why doesn't that make me feel any better?" Drum had grumbled.

We hadn't had many days to practice. We agreed that we'd keep it simple—that I'd stand in the middle, and Drum would circle around me and turn and dance a bit, looking like he was making me laugh. Then, together we'd do a circuit in step together like we were dancing, throw in a few sideways moves and some back steps, then end in front of the judges and bow—with Drum putting his front hooves out in front and bending down all cute for the ah factor. It seemed to work pretty well once Drummer had mastered the bow, and I was secretly confident that we'd be fine with me telling Drum what to do and where to go. But now we were here at the showground, and the tiny bit of cooperation I'd had from Drum seemed to be evaporating. I hoped he would see it through OK.

The field was buzzing with activity. In one corner was the dressage arena set out with white markers and the judge's car at one end. Flags announced the start of the cross-country course on the other side, and show jumping fences gleamed in yet another part. Horse trailers lined up in the adjacent field, and a big tent was surrounded by promotional banners for Sublime Equine, all in their familiar orange and lime colors. Glamorous girls in Sublime Equine outfits handed out Sublime Equine catalogs. We found a shady tree to claim as our own, and Katy and Bean went off to confirm our entry.

"Everyone looks alarmingly competent," said James, eyeing up one of the Sublime Equine promotional girls wearing a very tight polo shirt and jodhpurs. She had sparkly false eyelashes on, too. It was strange seeing James in his best riding clothes—tweed jacket, shirt and tie, and jodhpurs—instead of his more familiar torn jeans and scruffy boots. Moth's mane and tail were braided, and we'd all bullied James into trimming the feather off her four white stockings, which were whitened and encased in brushing boots. Her usual striped Indian blanket had been replaced by a neat white saddle blanket. She'd had a makeover, like my mom.

Bean, too, was dressed up in her show gear—blue jacket and hat with cream jodhpurs. Katy had her extra-purple cross-country colors on, and I, well, I had my usual jodhs and a T-shirt. My outfit was in my backpack.

"Mmmm. That team of chestnuts is a bit scary," I said.

"That group doesn't look so hot," James whispered, pointing. A team of assorted scary-looking ponies sauntered past. They weren't even very clean, and the riders all looked half asleep. "If we don't beat them, I'll eat my hat."

Suddenly, a streak of chestnut and white cantered past. It was Catriona on Bambi. Seeing us, Cat turned and rode over to chat. Well, she chatted to Bean, Katy, and James. Her friends.

"Who are you, and what have you done with James?" She laughed, referring to James's transformation. Then she

40

turned to me and her face and tone dropped. "I see you're here to make up the numbers."

"You won't say that when we're riding around with our blue ribbons," I snapped back. Then I wondered why on earth I'd said such a stupid thing.

"Fat chance!" sneared Cat. "We've got Scott Purnell on Warrior doing the cross-country, and India Hammond on the Dweeb as our show jumping entry—they're both the best." My heart sank. I'd met Scott briefly at school, and he had been interested in me talking to Warrior. But then he'd forgotten, or not bothered, which is hardly surprising as he's a couple of years older than me. Then I realized that it only left Cat to do the wild card event. She was in my group. Oh, pooh!

"Phew, I'm here!" a voice shouted. As Dee pushed her bike across to us, Cat turned Bambi and rode off. Even from the back she looked disdainful. How come she's so good at that?

"Oh, good, the groom's arrived," James said gleefully, throwing his reins at her. "Look after Moth, can you, Dee? I need to walk the jumping course."

"Oh, give me a second," pleaded Dee. "I'm in need of a drink after pedaling all that way."

Bluey was the first in our team to do his event, and we watched him quivering with excitement at the start of the cross-country, ready to get going, Katy a vision in purple.

"Good luck, Katy!" we all shouted. This was the start of our challenge attempt—how would it go? Katy grinned at us and I could hear Bluey psyching himself up.

"Come on, let me at 'em!" he hissed to himself. And when the starter shouted "*Go!*" Bluey bounded off in a canter, almost unseating Katy. We watched them leap over the first, bounce over the second, and then they were gone—disappearing with a purple flash into the woods to tackle the rest of the course.

"At least they'll be fine," said Bean. We all agreed with her. Bluey was our trump card, our one sure thing. It was the rest of us who needed help.

Sure enough, Bluey got a splendid clear with no time faults. Katy's face was one delighted grin—a good impression of a split melon.

"Oh, he was so wonderful," she gushed, sliding out of the saddle and throwing her arms around her pony's sweaty neck. Bluey looked all smug and breathless. "He just ate up all the jumps. He just so loves it!"

We all patted Bluey and told them both how great they were. Our Sublime Equine Challenge had got off to a flying start, and we all felt totally confident. This was going to be a piece of cake, I thought. Brookdale here we come! A big fat zero and Bluey's fast time was chalked up onto the scoreboard in the column next to Katy Harris and Blue Haze, Bluey's show name.

We all helped Bean get ready for the dressage and then stood in a supportive huddle as she rode Tiffany around to warm up. I didn't know what Bean was so worried about—she and Tiffany looked every inch a dressage pair, if you didn't count Tiff muttering about something spooky over there and a balloon behind her and what was that woman with the dog doing. Bean rides so well, and I could see them impressing the judges, much more than Drum and me anyway. Once she was in the arena, I was sure she'd be OK.

Leanne and Mr. Higgins had just done their test, and as they rode out and the next rider rode in, Leanne steered her dun gelding over to Bean, and we could see them talking, with Leanne pointing at Tiffany. As Leanne rode off we could tell something was wrong. Very wrong. Bean was close to tears. Stopping in front of us, she threw the reins onto her pony's golden neck, her shoulders slumped in defeat.

"We can't do this!" she said.

"Of course you can," said Katy, soothingly.

"You'll be fine," I said. "You were really great in practice."

"No, you don't get it, *we can't do this!*" Bean repeated, through clenched teeth.

"Why?" we all said.

"What did Leanne say?" asked James.

"Leanne knows the rules. She's just told me that all dressage entrants have to wear the right tack as stated in the rules, or they'll be disqualified—and that means the team will be disqualified, too."

"So what do you need?" I asked, running my eyes over Tiffany. "Is your bit wrong? It's just an eggbutt snaffle. You haven't got a martingale, which isn't allowed…what's the problem?"

"It's the noseband," said Bean, her bottom lip

trembling. "Tiffany has to wear a noseband—and you know what happens when she does. The whole team's out of the competition!"

CHAPTER 5

I STARED AT TIFFANY'S NAKED nose. Tiffany hadn't worn a noseband since I'd overheard her telling Bambi about her noseband phobia, something to do with an injury in her youth. Ever since the day I'd told Bean it was the noseband that made Tiffany shake her head uncontrollably, the offending piece of tack had been dumped. We were all so used to seeing Tiffany's naked face, we hadn't given it a second thought.

Until now.

"Why didn't Leanne say something at the yard?" asked James.

"She thought I was still doing the show jumping!" replied Bean. "We never do dressage! Not since the last time when I lost my way—that was way before you told me about Tiffany's noseband phobia, Pia."

"I'll get you Bluey's," Katy said, already running toward the ponies.

"That won't do any good!" grumbled Bean. "Tiff will just shake her head all the way around her test. At least it won't matter if I forget it!"

Sliding off her pony, she burst into tears. Horrified, I looked at James, who put his arm around her and said quietly, "Oh, come on, Bean, it'll be OK…"

"Don't, James!" Bean sniffed, pulling away. "I never wanted to do the dressage—no one cared how I felt, and now it's my fault we'll be disqualified."

Bean was right, we had pushed her into it and ignored her protests—we'd been so sure she'd been exaggerating and had focused only on how well she usually rode. How well she rode was immaterial if she couldn't remember the test, or Tiffany's headshaking returned.

Pushing James out of the way, I put my arm on Bean's shoulder, hoping she wouldn't turn on me. She didn't. "Bean, don't cry, please. I'll talk to Tiffany—she'll try her best for a few minutes, I'm sure."

Bean wiped her nose on her black jacket, leaving a nasty, snotty trail.

I got close to Tiffany and whispered in her ear. "Tiffany, don't freak, but you need to wear a noseband for the dressage test—it's just for a few minutes. Please, please, don't headshake! Poor Bean's really upset and it would mean a lot to her."

Tiffany turned and looked at me, the fear obvious in her eyes. "Please don't make me wear one. Please! I get flashbacks to when I had one on too tightly, before I was with Bean. It hurt so much. It just freaks me out."

"I know, but we really need you to do this. You can do it, I know you can. We'll put it on loosely—it's just a cavesson. Please try." A cavesson noseband doesn't actually do anything, it just hangs there. I didn't know why dressage rules state that horses and ponies have to wear something that does nothing, but it was too late to be challenging it now.

"What's she saying?" sniffed Bean, wrapping a supportive arm around her pony's neck.

I told her.

"Please, Tiffany—I don't want to do this either, but it's for the team," Bean whispered to her.

A breathless Katy arrived with Bluey's cavesson noseband, and we threaded it onto Tiffany's bridle. The palomino stiffened and held her breath as we did it up as loosely as we could.

"Promise me you'll get this off as soon as I come out!" Tiffany said.

"Of course, the very second you're finished," I promised.

"Poor Tiffany, I'm so, so sorry," sniffed Bean, mounting and heading for the arena just as the announcer called for Charlotte Beanie and Tiffany's Golden Trinket to the dressage arena.

We all held our breath.

The best parts of Bean and Tiffany's test were the start and finish. The stuff in between was worse than we could have imagined. Tiffany broke pace at canter and, unable to help herself, she shook her head violently several times. Bean, upset and trembling, forgot the test three times—just as she promised she would—and left a whole chunk out altogether.

"Well done!" we all chimed loyally, trying to be supportive as they came out. I rushed to strip the noseband off Tiffany's bridle.

"Oh, that was awful." Tiffany shuddered. She had obviously been very brave about it, considering.

Dressage is scored as a percentage—anything over 60 percent is considered pretty darn good. Each movement is marked out of ten, with the percentage worked out later, and Bean obviously lost quite a number of points for not completing several of the required movements.

"Thirty-two percent!" wailed Bean when she read her score on the board. "It must have looked even worse than it felt."

"Don't worry, we can drop your score," said James tactlessly.

"I think you did great, under the circumstances," Katy said firmly, and we all agreed. Secretly, I could see our chances of qualifying for the final at this event racing downhill. Fast.

I couldn't help noticing that Leanne had scored 79 percent, a fantastic score and in the lead so far. We went back to the ponies to nurse our hurts. Bean's dressage score was a blow, but we couldn't do anything about it. It wasn't like she hadn't warned us. We had insisted she'd be all right. We'd been wrong. OK, we could drop her score, but it put a lot of pressure on the rest of the team to do well.

"You and Moth had better leave all the jumps up after taking the event from Bean," I warned James.

"Thank goodness you're all back!" said Dee, tangled up in reins. "Perhaps now I can go to the bathroom. Can you *not* leave me three ponies all at once? How did Tiffany and Bean do? Was the noseband all right?"

"No!" said Bean, telling Dee all about it. It was strange hearing someone whining to Dee for a change.

When it was James's turn to jump, Bean and I followed him over to the arena, leaving Katy and Dee with the ponies. India Hammond from Team SLIC was flying around the course on the Dweeb, her careful, flea-bitten gray pony. Blond and very pretty, India looked every inch the part in her navy jacket and pink tie.

"She's really good," hissed Bean. "She's been show jumping since she was tiny."

I could hear the Dweeb talking himself around the course: "Hang on, India, this is a tricky one, now this fence, yes! Where to now? Oh, I see, the wall, here we go, toes tucked up…"

I noticed James gazing at India. Well, she was a bit of a stunner. I couldn't help feeling a pang of jealousy, and I wished I looked like India, blond and petite, instead of having a mane of unruly reddish brown hair that matched Drummer's coat. When India rode past us after her faultless clear round, she smiled at James and waved. We watched her ride back to her teammates, who all clapped her on the back and cheered.

For the Sublime Equine Challenge, there was to be no jump-off—everyone had to aim for a fast clear round. Every fence down added ten seconds to the round, so accuracy was vital. James and Moth did not copy India's example. Although fast, Moth clipped a pole, and then she managed to dislodge a brick in the wall, adding twenty seconds to her time and putting her way down the line. We weren't exactly shining.

"Never mind," I said to James, who was all apologetic. "You did your best."

"I think I'm still making poor Moth drop her hind legs," James said, hanging his head.

It was my turn. Could I make up some lost ground for the team?

"Go out and knock the judges dead!" whispered James, as I got Drummer dressed up in his red and yellow outfit. Epona was firmly zipped into my jodhpurs pocket. Our whole routine depended on her being with us.

"I'll never forgive you for this," hissed Drummer.

"Oh, don't be so melodramatic!" I told him, tying the ear protectors to his halter. "Four minutes, that's all!"

I gave James the CD of medieval-sounding lute and pianoforte music for my routine and he went over to give it to the steward. Luckily, with so many events going on, there was hardly anyone around the wild card ring, which was a huge relief. I dragged Drummer over and as we got there, I could see Cat performing her routine with Bambi.

Cat was long-reining her skewbald mare. She'd threaded two long lines through the stirrups on Bambi's saddle and was steering Bambi around in circles and figure eights. Then she got Bambi going sideways, and then backward. To finish, Bambi stood up straight in front of the judges and Cat came up beside her and saluted. It looked very precise and impressive, with Cat in her riding clothes and Bambi with her white patches gleaming, her chestnut patches shining in the sun, her mane and tail fiercely braided.

My heart sank. Why hadn't I thought of something as classy as that? Why had I thought up something that made me and Drummer look like fools? Our routine suddenly seemed childish, and I wished with all my heart that we didn't have to go in and perform it. Drum had been right all along. It was a stupid, stupid routine. What had I been thinking of in my amateurish homemade dress and wimple? This challenge thing was turning into a nightmare. Why had we ever thought it was a good idea? How had we expected to do well? What had we been thinking?

"It's your turn. Break a leg," whispered James, giving me a push. We had to pass Cat and Bambi as we jingle-jangled our way to the middle of the ring, and I heard Cat snort with laughter when she caught sight of us.

Oh, double pooh.

"Come on." Drum sighed. "Let's get it over with."

I nodded to the judges and one of them started the CD.

"OK, Drum, let's give it our all!" I whispered to him as the music blared out. Boy, it was loud. We'd never had it on that loud at home when we'd been practicing.

"OK, circle around me," I said to Drum.

"What?" Drummer said, planted to the spot.

"Circle around me!" I said louder.

"You'll have to speak up!" shouted Drummer, shaking his head and ringing all the bells.

51

"Just do what we did at home!" I yelled.

"I can't hear you!" Drummer replied.

It was hopeless! The combination of the music and Drum's ear protectors with bells on made it impossible for him to hear my direction. Somehow, we muddled through, but it wasn't anything like as polished as it had been in practice at home in the paddock. We went wrong, we turned away when we should have turned toward each other, and we finished at different times before the music stopped, bowing out of sync. I couldn't wait to get out of the arena.

"Thank you!" shouted one of the judges in a bored voice, obviously relieved that our performance was over.

We came third from last.

"Drum couldn't hear me," I explained.

"Maybe you should take those ear things off," suggested Dee.

"Good idea!" snorted Drummer.

"Oh, you heard that all right!" I said crossly.

"Well, there's no music thundering out like we're at Woodstock!" he replied. "With all these bells ringing, maybe you should think of adapting our routine—how about we change it to *The Hunchback of Notre Dame?* You could stuff a cushion up the back of your dress."

"It just needs adapting, that's all," Katy told me, unaware of Drummer's comments. "And we *all* need to practice a bit more. I mean, we didn't think we were going to win, did we?"

I remembered my boast to Cat about blue ribbons. Then I saw her on Bambi. A yellow ribbon fluttered from Bambi's bridle.

"Oh, look," said Bean. "Leanne and Cat's team has come in third." She rode Tiffany over and was soon congratulating Cat, who was beaming. I could hear Tiffany and Bambi talking—they're good chums and often graze in the field together.

"You did well!" said Tiffany.

"Yes, we've got a strong team. How's your team panning out?"

"Mmmm, well, you know what it's like, the humans are all keen so you have to put up a bit of a show, don't you? I don't really do dressage, as you know, *and* it turns out I have to wear a noseband, which is the final straw and—oh, *what's that?* Oh, it's OK, it's just a burger wrapper—so I'm hoping—well, Drum, Moth, and I all are—that we don't go through to the finals, especially as we don't get much in the way of thanks from anyone. It's all about them, them, them. We'd love to nip the whole thing—*look out*…oh, no, it's all right, it's just a small child with an ice cream—in the bud right here. Of course, we can't get Bluey onboard, he won't mess up the cross-country whatever you say to him. Oh, by the way, Drummer keeps asking me to put in a good word for him."

"Oh, don't remind me. He's such a pain. As if I'm going to fall for a bay who wears bells on his ears!"

"You are hard on him—he's OK really. But who's that gorgeous black creature on your team, the one who's doing the cross-country?"

"You mean Warrior? Mmmm, he is yummy, isn't he? I wouldn't mind if *he* liked me. I don't think I'm his type—he might go for you though. All blond and skinny."

Shutting my ears to their conversation, I took all Drummer's jester costume off. He shook himself and sneezed.

"Can we go home now?"

"I know what you're doing—you and Moth and Tiffany," I said menacingly.

"Don't know what you're talking about!"

We rode home in gloomy silence. Only Bluey was happy—as he always is when he's jumped a cross-country round. I could hear him talking the other ponies through it, jump by jump. The other ponies were bored into silence.

"You know that Leanne and Cat are halfway to qualifying, don't you?" said Bean.

"Yes, thank you, we know," I said.

"That cruddy team, the one with the funny-looking ponies and the grungy riders, they came in second. *Second!*" wailed James.

"Serves us right for underestimating them," said Katy. "What do you want with your hat, James? Fries? Salad?"

"Oh, you're funny!" said James.

"It's not even worth bothering to go to another qualifier," mumbled Bean.

"Of course it is!" said Katy.

"You would say that, you did really well. The rest of us are terrible," I reminded her.

"You've got a good routine," said James. "It just needs a few tweaks."

"No one liked it. Everyone laughed," I complained.

"I'll work the CD player next time. And if you make some adjustments to Drum's ear covers so he can hear you, that will fix it!"

"Yes, Pia," added Bean, "you're the only one who can do it—although I don't see how Tiff and I can do another dressage test in a noseband. It's impossible!"

"It's not only the noseband that's the trouble," said James. "You lost your way twice." I cringed. Talk about tactless.

"I can't remember dressage tests—I told you all that," Bean said with exaggerated calm, keeping her cool.

"I can," I said desperately, wondering if it wasn't too late to swap events with Bean. It was as if Katy could read my mind.

"We can't change events halfway through. The rules say the same team members have to do the same events throughout the competition. We just have to try harder next time," she said. As Katy was the only member of our team who'd been any good and, it appeared, had bothered to read the rules, we couldn't really argue.

"It's a shame you didn't know the rule about the noseband," James muttered.

"We weren't exactly Team Tremendous, were we?" grumbled Bean.

"Team Useless, more like," agreed James. "Perhaps we should call ourselves Team Desperate, or Team Argument, or Team Only-Here-to-Make-Up-the-Numbers!"

"Oh, that's the spirit!" said Katy sarcastically.

"It doesn't matter how hard we try if the ponies aren't onboard," I said, and relayed Tiffany and Bambi's conversation.

"Oh!" said Katy, lost for words for once.

"Well," I said grimly, "we only have one more chance to stay in the competition. If we don't place in the first three in the next qualifier, the decision will be taken away from us. We'll be out, whether we like it or not!"

CHAPTER 6

THAT EVENING, I MET Mom's new boyfriend, Greg. With the day having gone so badly, I wasn't in the mood to show myself off as the model daughter.

"This is Pia," said Mom. "Pia, I'd like you to meet Greg."

"Good evening, Pia."

"Umm, hello," I mumbled. Greg was pretty tall. He had sandy-colored hair, the sort of hair that looks like cotton balls, sort of undefined strands, just stuck on his head in a blob, like doll hair. His beard was gray and short and trimmed. His left earlobe sported a silver stud, which he was, like, decades too old for. What was that about?

"Pia's been looking forward to meeting you," Mom lied. I smiled. Well, it seemed expected.

"I understand you have a pony," said Greg. "I used to ride when I was younger, but I gave it up when I discovered girls." He looked across at Mom and grinned at her. She giggled back, blushing. I didn't really think I could handle all this after the day I'd had. I thought furiously for something to say. What do grown-ups say when they meet?

"What do you do for a living, Greg?"

"I'm a teacher. English. Do you enjoy English at school, Pia?"

OK, you can think I'm negative if you want (some of Drummer's attitude rubs off), but don't you think that teachers just never give it a rest? I mean, they just have to be right all the time, don't they? I prayed that Greg wasn't a typical teacher, because I could see trouble coming. It wasn't long before it started.

"Greg and I went to a fabulous restaurant by the river— I must take you there, Pia, you'd love it. Such a pretty place," Mom told me.

"Can you remember the name of the river, Sue?" Greg asked with a smarmy smile. "I did tell you."

See what I mean? "My mom's a grown-up!" I wanted to scream. "She wasn't on a field trip—it was a date, for goodness sake!"

"Oh, no, I can't. Sorry!" Mom giggled.

"It's detention for you, young lady!" joked Greg.

Pass the barf bag, I thought. Luckily, they left soon after for dinner at some restaurant Mom has always liked the look of. As soon as they'd gone, I called Bean.

"Look," I said as soon as she answered, "we have to have a powwow tomorrow at the yard and discuss where the team goes from here. I think I need to have a word with the ponies. See you there at nine?"

"OK, sounds like a plan," Bean said. "What are you doing now? There's a great movie on in ten minutes."

"My mom's just gone on a date," I told her. "You wouldn't believe the geek she's seeing now. Can you call Katy and tell her about tomorrow? I'll call James."

James wasn't answering his cell, so I sent him a text message. Then I cooked myself a baked potato with cheese and beans, watched the movie Bean had recommended, which made me laugh despite our disastrous day, and took myself off to bed before Greg brought Mom home. I couldn't face another dose of him.

The next morning, Mom insisted on asking my opinion of Greg. I so hate the postmortem of the first meeting. Remembering I had promised to support her in her dating, I put on my ever-so-sincere-if-you-don't-look-too-close face that I've had rather a lot of practice at recently.

"What's important, Mom, is that you like him."

"I do, he's very attentive."

I didn't want to think about Greg being attentive to my mom. I biked to the yard with Epona in my pocket, trying to put all unbidden images out of my mind. Katy and Bean were already there so we pulled all the ponies in from the field, including Moth.

"Are you going to read them the riot act?" asked Bean.

"That's the plan!" I told her grimly. Towing the ponies in behind us, we found James had arrived.

"Come on," I said, "let's take this bunch somewhere where we won't be disturbed."

"What are we going to do?" he joked. "Give them a good thrashing?"

"Don't say that!" cried Katy, hugging Bluey protectively. As if we would!

"Oh, come on, Katy, it was a joke," said James. "I don't even carry a whip on Moth, you know that!"

"It wasn't funny!" said Katy, furious with James.

We took them all behind Bambi's, Drummer's, and Moth's stables. Unfortunately, there was a lot of grass growing there.

"Oooh, this is the sort of telling off I like!" cried Drum, dropping his head to graze. Tiffany and Bluey followed his lead, only Moth stood all polite as usual, waiting for James to tell her it was all right to do the same.

I hauled Drummer's head up. "Now look, you guys," I began, "we know you're not making any effort with this Sublime Equine Challenge."

"That's not fair!" wailed Bluey.

"Oh, sorry, Bluey," I said. "I know you are. You're the exception. Your friends here are deliberately sabotaging any effort to qualify in an effort to cut down on work."

"Are you?" asked Bluey, in wide-eyed amazement. He is such an honest pony.

"Oh, come on," said Drummer, defensively. "I was dressed up to look like the village idiot. No wonder I'm not excited."

"I wore the noseband under duress, and I take exception to your accusations," Tiffany said huffily. "Is that a...oh, no, it's just an old bucket!" she added, her indignation in ruins.

"Yes, you did," I agreed. "But I heard you talking with Bambi. You can't deny it!"

"What's she saying?" said Bean.

Moth said nothing. As usual. I couldn't give Epona to

James with Bean and Katy there. He would have to get her feedback later.

"How could you not try?" asked Bluey, looking crestfallen. "I jumped my heart out for the team."

Tiffany shifted her hooves, and Drummer looked into the distance. Then Tiffany grunted and spoke.

"Actually," she said huffily, "Drum and I think we're being taken for granted."

"What do you mean?" I said baffled.

"What are they saying?" Bean asked again.

"That's right," interrupted Drummer. "You want us to do these things, but do we hear any word of thanks? Any praise? No! It's just complain, complain, complain. Katy's always appreciative of Bluey's hard work, and you can see the result for yourselves."

I was stunned.

"What's the news?" James said. "Come on, Pia, tell us!"

"Er…" I didn't know where to start. A very uncomfortable feeling grew in my stomach. It got worse and worse. Drum was right, I hadn't given him any encouragement at all—I had just grumbled and complained all the time. I felt really ashamed. I took a deep breath.

"It's our fault," I told the others.

"Ours? How?" Bean asked.

"Why?" said James.

"They say they never get any thanks for their efforts, that we don't appreciate them. We just whine."

There was a stunned silence.

"Oh, Bluey, I'm sorry!" said Katy, throwing her arms around his neck and smothering him with kisses.

"Actually, Katy, the ponies say you're the only one who's OK. And you are."

"You are really nice to Bluey," added Bean thoughtfully. "And positive."

"Looks like it's up to us to change things," said James.

"I'm so sorry, Tiff," said Bean, stroking Tiffany's golden neck. "I promise I'll be more like Katy."

"That will be nice," sniffed Tiffany. "I'll try harder, too—even with the noseband if I have to."

"She's going all out next time," I assured Bean.

"Oh, good girl, have all the grass you want!" cried Bean, patting Tiffany's neck like mad. I turned to Drummer.

"I'm really sorry, Drum. You're right, and I've been totally in the wrong. Can we start again?"

Drummer looked at Bluey and Tiffany, and then me. He gave a huge sigh. "Oh, OK, I'll be magnificent next time," he said. "I'll perform like Trigger, or Champion the Wonder Horse. I'll be so amazing; I'll be nominated for an Oscar. Now can I get my head down before that greedy Tiffany eats all this grass?"

"Go to town!" I told him.

When the grass looked like a flock of sheep had spent the night there, we took the ponies back to their stables, and I handed Epona to James when no one was looking.

"Your turn to have a word, find out Moth's take on it all," I told him. Five minutes later and James was back.

"We're good," he said. "Moth's jumping faults were genuine, but I could be a bit more thankful, too, apparently. She said we have to remember we're a team."

I felt so utterly guilty. How awful to be reminded by our own ponies about how we were supposed to get the most out of them. In our excitement and nervousness about the Sublime Equine Challenge, we'd overlooked the fact that ponies, just like people, respond to praise and encouragement, not negativity. We so totally had to remember that and stop whining all the time.

Drummer and I practiced our routine again, and I made sure I was much more polite and asked his opinion on certain movements. He even had some good suggestions. Tiffany and Bean did some schooling (minus the noseband!) with Katy, and James offering useful advice from the fence and they made a real fuss over Tiff. Both ponies were cooperation personified. It was so great! In the afternoon, we all went for a fast, hard ride in the woods to let off some steam. The ponies loved it, and so did we!

"OK," said James, pulling an overexcited Moth up after we'd raced one another to the lake, "we're good to go all-out at the next qualifier. Let's go for it!"

We all gave a high five and whooped with delight. Bring it on! We were so going to do better the next time around. The ponies' pep talk had definitely straightened us all out!

We rode back to the yard with Tiffany, now thoroughly excited, going sideways and setting Drum off. It took forever to settle them down, and as we walked through the woods, Katy brought up the subject of our team name, insisting it would help the team spirit.

"I don't get Cat and Leanne's team name," said Bean. "I mean SLIC, what does that mean?"

"It's their names—Scott, Leanne, India, and Catriona," Katy explained.

I thought that was clever—and lucky that it worked.

"Well, we could do that. How about we're Team BPKJ?" suggested Bean.

"That's gibberish!" snorted Katy.

"That's it, Team Gibberish!" yelled James.

"I think we need to come up with something snappy. Something that sums up what we're about," Katy said.

"So we're back to Team Useless," said James. Katy glared at him.

"Or we could be ironic," James said. "How about the Fantastic Four?"

"That's not ironic," said Bean. "That's just lying."

"But maybe if we give ourselves something to live up to, it might not turn out ironic at all," suggested Katy.

"As long as we don't have T-shirts," I said. "I don't want to walk around with that on my back."

"Can anyone think of anything better?" asked James.

No one said a word.

"That's it then, the Fantastic Four it is!" said Katy, as we rode into the yard.

"Excuse me," said a voice. It was Drummer and he wasn't

very happy. "There are eight of us in this team. I can see our little pep talk has had very little effect."

"What's your point?" I said confused. I could see Katy and Bean looking at me. James had ridden off to Moth's stable and was out of earshot.

"Yes," added Tiffany, "what about us?"

"You're doing it again," said Bluey, shaking his head.

"What's wrong now?" Katy asked.

"We can't be the Fantastic Four," I told her. "There are eight of us."

Bean's hand flew to her mouth. "Oh, no, we're in trouble again!" she cried.

"Oh, sorry, Bluey. You're right!" exclaimed Katy.

"Can we be the Fantastic Eight, then?" I asked. It didn't sound as catchy.

"Hardly," said Drummer, in disgust.

"We can be the Great Eight," suggested Bluey.

"Perfect!" I said, and told the others. They agreed, and Bean trotted Tiffany over to tell James there'd been a change of plan. Already!

As I took my feet out of my stirrups, my cell phone went off. Sliding to the ground, I saw it was Dad calling. We hadn't spoken for a while.

"Hi, Dad!" I said.

"Hello, Pumpkin—how's my best girl?" he boomed. I had to hold the phone at arm's length, he was so loud.

"OK, thanks. How are you. And Lyn?" I remembered to add.

"Yes, we're fine. Thanks, love. We'd love to come and see you—and hey, you'll love this…"

I held my breath.

"Lyn's taking up horse riding."

There was a pause for dramatic effect. I said nothing—due to the fact that I was totally stunned, my mouth wide open like a landed fish.

"I said she might as well try it out on old Drummer before she gets all the gear in case she doesn't like it," Dad continued. "We'd love to come over tomorrow, and Lyn can have a ride on Drummer. What do you say?"

Skinny Lynny on Drummer? Don't think so! But then, I could hardly say no, could I? I got my gaping mouth working again and went to say OK, but it came out as a sort of mouse squeak.

"Right, it's a date!" said Dad. He never seems to understand that I might have plans. It's as though I'd been moping around, with nothing to do, just waiting for him to call so I can let his horrible, skinny girlfriend ride MY pony. Then I remembered that I'd promised myself to make an effort with Skinny Lynny, and what had I just learned from the ponies?

"Er…" I said.

"We'll meet you at Drummer's at eleven o'clock tomorrow. I'm looking forward to seeing you, Pumpkin. We both are!"

He hung up.

"Did I hear right?" inquired a wide-eyed Drummer, his

head up like an indignant llama. "Do I take it I'm giving pony rides tomorrow?"

"Yes," I told him. "And before you get all huffy about it, remember that my dad pays for your keep so play ball or you could find yourself in one of the classified ads in the local paper."

"No need for threats," Drummer sniffed. "I knew your positivity wouldn't last."

Oh, pooh, I thought. It seemed no sooner had we fixed on one problem, another galloped up to fill its space.

CHAPTER 7

IT WAS ALMOST A quarter to twelve when they arrived. I'd had Drummer tacked up for over half an hour. You can imagine how he felt about that!

"Hi there, Pumpkin!" shouted Dad, once he'd parked the car next to Sophie's luxury horse trailer. I'm probably getting a bit old to be called that. I mean, it had been OK when I was six. Would Dad still be calling me Pumpkin when I was sixteen, or eighteen, or really old, say twenty-one?

When Skinny Lynny got out of the car I couldn't stop my mouth from becoming a black hole. She was wearing bronze-colored breeches and the latest Sublime Equine lime-green polo shirt. Long, leather riding boots made her walk as though she had no knees and her long, blond hair spilled out from under a top-of-the-range blue velvet riding hat. I thought this session on Drum was a tryout to decide whether she was going to take up riding? She looked fairly committed to me. At least four-hundred-dollars committed, and my dad would have paid for it. I heard a gulp behind me.

"Check her out!" Drummer exclaimed. "I thought you said she couldn't ride?"

"She can't!" I hissed back.

"Doesn't Lyn look the part, eh?" said Dad, looking all pleased and proud with his trophy girlfriend in her over-the-top getup.

"I thought you'd look a bit nicer, Pia," scolded Lyn, looking me up and down. Rude! I was dressed in jodhpurs and a polo shirt.

"I think I might enjoy this." Drummer chuckled.

"Drummer…" I growled in a warning voice. Skinny Lynny tipped her head to one side and smiled.

"Dear Pia," she said in the sort of voice you use to tell tiny children that their teddy bears will cry if they don't eat up all their greens, "are the ponies talking to you again?"

Skinny Lynny had never really believed that I could hear what horses and ponies were saying. She'd always treated me as though I was making it up, or I was bonkers. I didn't really care whether she believed me or not. Impressing Skinny Lynny wasn't a priority of mine.

"Now," said Dad, rubbing his hands together, "I can't wait to see the future show jumper of the year onboard."

I led Drummer to the outdoor school and over to the mounting block, showing Skinny Lynny how to mount, and after a few squeaks and squeals, and a shove from me, she was soon sitting in Drum's saddle, looking scared stiff.

"It's very high up," she said.

"No, it isn't," I mumbled sulkily.

"You look fantastic in the saddle, darling," shouted Dad from the other side of the fence.

"No, she doesn't," I argued. Skinny Lynny sat stiffly with her bottom jutting out and her heels clamped into Drummer's sides.

"Now sit up and tuck your tail under you," I told her.

"I haven't got a tail," said Skinny Lynny, breathless at the suggestion.

"I know, but make like you do. That's better. Now breathe."

"Oh, I was holding my breath!" gasped Skinny Lynny. "How did you know that?"

"All beginners do it. OK, don't rest your hands on the saddle; carry them like this…Good. Now put all your weight down your legs and into your heels. Let them drop. Relax…" I wobbled her legs until they softened. "Now I'm going to lead Drum around and I want you to stay in that position."

Drum took a step forward. Skinny Lynny squealed. I just spotted the wicked gleam in his eye as Drum shook his head, which had Skinny Lynny clutching his mane, squeaking like a guinea pig.

This wasn't going well.

"Don't squeal, you'll scare Drummer," I said. Skinny Lynny looked at me wide-eyed and terrified. "It's OK, he's not easily scared," I reassured her. "But you need to be quiet."

"Will he throw me off?" she whispered.

I so wanted to say yes. Instead, I said, "No, no, he's a pussycat, honestly!" as Drummer—encouraged by the success of his head shaking—put in a hop and squealed himself. Skinny Lynny squeaked and yelled, "Make him stop or I'll get off!"

"Oh, this is going to be such fun," sniggered Drummer. Secretly, I agreed with him. Skinny was hopeless. I mean, we'd only taken three tiny steps and she was all for throwing in the towel.

"Just sit up and Drummer will be fine," I told her. "Honestly, I won't let go of him."

Dad climbed through the fence and came over.

"Are you all right, darling?" he said, all concerned. He wasn't talking to me.

"This horse is dangerous," Skinny replied accusingly, "and Pia can't control him."

"Of course he isn't, and of course I can," I said.

"I could be!" threatened Drummer menacingly.

"Come on, Lyn, you've got all the gear now. You might at least walk around," Dad encouraged.

"Well, I'll try to be brave," Skinny Lynny replied, smiling at Dad.

"That's my girl!" beamed Dad. I thought I was going to throw up. I mean, it was hardly heroic, plodding around with me hanging on to Drummer's reins.

So we walked around, and the squeaking died down— at least it did from the saddle. Drum had realized he was onto a good thing, however, and as soon as I took my eye off him, he put in a hop, or he threw his head down to scratch his knee, or he shook his head and squealed.

Every time, Skinny Lynny clutched his mane and caught her breath or she squealed back. It was like the clash of the squeaky toys.

"Shall we try a trot?" I said wearily.

"Is that fast?" Skinny gasped.

"Fast-er," I said.

"Oh, OK, second gear. All right," she agreed. I explained what trotting would feel like and got her to hold the front of the saddle.

"Keep your heels down and sit up tall," I said. "Here we go—nice and gently!" I growled at Drummer.

"Hee-hee!" Drum chuckled, and he bounded forward into trot. Skinny yelled for him to stop, stop, *stop!* And Drum obliged, very suddenly, snorting when Skinny landed on his neck.

"Trotting's awful!" She gulped. "How can this be so difficult—it looks so easy!"

"Yeah, well, everyone thinks that, but it takes a long time to learn," I said. "You want to try again, now you know what to expect?"

We did. We even managed half a circuit in trot. After that, I decided to stick to walking and got Skinny Lynny to steer instead. That went rather well, and Skinny Lynny managed a smile. Once she'd learned how to stop, she was much more confident.

"Come on, now," Dad called, already bored. "We don't want to be late for lunch, Lyn." I remembered that he'd never been very interested in watching me ride either.

"Oh, hold on," said Drummer, and he lifted his tail and dropped a large poop on the sand.

"Oh, that's so awful!" whined drama queen Skinny, dropping one rein and wafting her hand in front of her face.

"It's only pony poo," I muttered.

I got Skinny Lynny to lead Drummer back to the yard. Of course, he grabbed hold of the bit and dragged her over to the feed room, and I had to rescue her. Then he rubbed his head on her, leaving brown hairs all over the lime-green Sublime Equine polo top, and concluded by scoring a direct hit on her foot with his near front hoof, offering Skinny Lynny yet another screaming opportunity.

"Oops!" exclaimed Drummer, all innocent.

"I don't know that Drummer is a very safe pony for you, Pia," mused Dad, nursing Skinny Lynny's foot. "He seems a bit wild. I can get you a quieter pony, if you like."

"Of course Drummer isn't wild," I told him. "Honestly, Dad, he's just playing up because he knows Lyn isn't very experienced. All ponies do it."

"Well, if you change your mind…" Dad continued.

"Stop it!" I hissed, looking Drummer in the eye. "I know what you're doing, but it'll backfire on you. She's not an Xbox game."

"I don't know how you put up with the awful horsey smell around here," said Skinny Lynny, screwing up her nose.

"Horses smell OK!" I said.

"But all that manure—from the muck heap. I mean, it's steaming," said Skinny. "It can't be healthy."

"It's fine. No one notices it after a while," I said firmly. Now she was going to get Drum sold on the grounds of health and safety. Honestly!

"If you think that's bad…" began Drummer, lifting his tail and letting out a long, and very smelly, fart. Skinny put her hand over her nose and whimpered. I couldn't understand it—I mean, she lives with my dad and he's much worse than Drum when he's had Mexican.

"Well, good-bye, Drummer. Thank you for the ride," Skinny Lynny said, patting Drummer on the forehead. Drum blinked dramatically every time her hand connected. Pat-blink, pat-blink, pat-blink.

"Bye-bye, Lyn!" Skinny Lynny said in a pretend Drummer voice. "Come and ride me again soon!"

"Oh, puh-leeese!" said Drummer, rolling his eyes and backing into his box to escape.

Skinny wiped her hands on a nearby bale of hay, anxious to get any Drummer-scent and Drummer-dirt off them. I don't know why, Drum smells great—when he's not farting.

We went out for lunch. And, get this, Skinny Lynny didn't even get hat hair! Peeling off her riding hat, she just shook her head and looked gorgeous. How does that work? When I take my riding hat off, my hair's stuck to my head like it's been glued.

All the men in the pub swiveled around to stare at Skinny in her breeches and boots. I could see Dad puffing out his chest in pride, like he was personally responsible for

Skinny's figure. I suppose that's why he ran off with her in the first place. The thought of my dad behaving like those lecherous men made me feel a bit strange. I mean, yuck!

"So what's on your agenda this summer vacation, Pia?" asked Dad. I told them about the Sublime Equine Challenge, and how Drum and I were the wild card. I sort of glossed over how badly our team had performed in the first qualifier, concentrating instead on our plans to get to the Brookdale final.

After lunch, Dad dropped me back at the yard. "We'll have to do this again," he said.

"Mmmm," agreed Skinny. "Now that I've got all the gear, I'll need to use it!"

I waved and sighed with relief as I watched the car bounce down the drive and away. Then I remembered how I had promised myself I'd make an effort with Skinny Lynny.

And how I had failed.

Again.

CHAPTER 8

HAVING HAD OUR CONFIDENCE shaken so much at the first qualifier, we were all very nervous at the second, held at Beeches Riding School, even though the ponies had promised to do their best, and we were all determined to make them feel good whatever the outcome. If we didn't make the first three this time, it was the end of the road as far as our Brookdale ambitions went.

Beeches was miles away, so by the time we'd ridden over there, we were all pretty well warmed up. I had our outfits in my backpack, so they were a bit creased, but we had to go with it. I wished I'd asked Dee to bring them with her—her mom was dropping her off by car after her schooling session with Dolly. Her HOYS campaign was in full swing, and she'd just missed qualifying at her last show by one place. Not for anything would I have swapped places with Dee in the horse trailer on the return journey with her miffed mom. Can you imagine?

This time, Drum and I were first to go in the wild card event. As I waited in the collecting ring, trying not to look at the other teams and smoothing down the creases in my skirt, I whispered to Drummer, reminding him of his promise.

"Stop worrying," he said. "I'll be an absolute pro. Honest. Your wimple's wonky, by the way—you're letting me down."

I pulled the conical hat straight. There was a stiff breeze, and the chiffon scarf kept blowing across my face. My yellow dress threatened to trip me up. I saw Katy, Bean, Dee-Dee with Bluey, and Tiffany and Moth, all grinning and giving me the thumbs-up sign. Well, the humans were. The ponies couldn't because they don't have thumbs, obviously.

"The next competitors are Pia Edwards and Drummer, for the Great Eight," the announcer managed to say without sniggering, which was impressive. Drum and I walked into the ring and faced the judges—three of them standing with clipboards, looking all stern and important. I nodded toward James and he started the CD player. It was now or never!

Drummer was as good as his word. He twirled, he shuffled, he did exactly what we'd practiced and what I asked him to do. He even shook his head a couple of times to get the bells going. At the end, we bowed to the judges, and I could see them all smiling broadly—they even clapped.

"You *star!*" I hissed to Drummer, patting him like crazy as we left the ring.

"Told you," he said smugly.

"Oh, well done, you were both amazing!" squealed Katy, peeling off Drum's leg bandages.

"Good old Drummer!" cried Dee-Dee, forcing pony cubes into my pony's willing mouth.

"Hey! Lay off the 'old' part," Drummer mumbled, shaking his head as I peeled off his ear protectors.

"Good job, Pia!" said James.

"Now you all have to be fabulous, too!" I laughed, relieved our part was over. It was a tremendous start. Our score was a decent fourteen out of twenty. Not bad!

I caught sight of Cat and Bambi performing their polished routine, their teammates cheering at the end. But we couldn't stay long, because it was Bean's turn to perform her dressage.

"I'm so nervous. Look!" she said, thrusting wobbly hands out in front of her. "What if we mess up again? I'll let you all down. What if I let Tiffany down? She's been so fantastic lately—and she's been so brave about the noseband."

"Just do your best," said Katy, patting Bean's arm.

"You looked great at the last practice," said Dee-Dee.

"Oh, why couldn't you do the dressage?" whimpered Bean. "Dolly would just walk it."

"OK, you go to shows with my mom," offered Dee.

Bean pulled a face at her. Suddenly the dressage didn't seem so bad after all.

"Just do your best, that's all we ask," said James. "No one is going to blame you if you don't do well."

"Oh, my legs are shaking so much, I don't think I can mount Tiffany," moaned Bean.

We all shoved her into the saddle, and I glanced at Tiffany. "Don't worry," she said huffily, "I'm going for it this time." She gulped. "Is it time for the noseband?"

As we threaded the noseband on at the very last minute, Tiffany closed her eyes and swallowed hard. She really did hate it. I had to admire her courage—but could she get past her bad memories? And could Bean remember the test?

Tiffany pulled out all the stops and did a good test with only half a head shake. Bean managed to hold it together through a few wobbly moments when we could see she wasn't sure whether to make a transition or turn across the arena. She still went wrong though. Twice.

When Bean finished her test, we crowded around her making encouraging noises.

"Why am I so bad at dressage?" she cried, dismounting and ripping off the noseband before giving Tiffany some polo mints. Tiffany rubbed her nose across Bean's shoulder as if to rub away the memory of the hated noseband. "I was so much better at home—I just can't remember anything when it's a competition."

Their score was 41 percent—better than last time but still pretty terrible. No one else had a score less than 57 percent. Gloomily, we all regrouped at a tree we'd picked out. Although there was a breeze, the sun was strong, and we tied the ponies up to some string we'd tied around the trunk and had a break.

"My mom should be here any minute," James said, looking at his watch. "She's bringing some lunch."

Now that my part was over I was ravenous, and I'd been eyeing up the burger van. I wondered what James's mom would be like. When I'd first moved to Laurel Farm, James's scruffy appearance had so fired my imagination, I'd believed him to be some kind of gypsy prince. After hearing that his parents had bought him Moth at the drop of a hat, I'd had an instant rethink. I'd seen his dad—he often dropped James off at the stables in his (expensive-looking) car, but I'd yet to meet his mom.

Petite, blond, expensively dressed, James's mom looked chic, young, and very, very glamorous, like an ex-model or something. James ran to help her carry the huge cooler she had brought along, and she opened it up and invited us all to dig in. There were sandwiches, sausage rolls, hard-boiled eggs, and chips, then éclairs, doughnuts, cheesecakes—and cans of Coke underneath. Dee-Dee, Bean, and I stuffed ourselves, and Katy and James made us save some for them to eat later—they were feeling too nervous to tackle anything now.

"I'll only bring it back up again," Katy told us.

"Yuck, don't waste it!" Bean exclaimed, cramming another doughnut into her mouth, happier now her part in the challenge was over.

"Oh, James," I yelled, "you've only got ten minutes to warm up!"

Tightening his girth, James leaped into Moth's saddle and headed for the show jumping ring at a fast trot. Katy volunteered to stay with the ponies, so the rest of us, together with James's mom, followed him over. As we walked across the grass, James's mom fell in step with me.

"James thinks very highly of you, Pia. He says you've helped him a lot with Moth," she said, smiling.

"Oh, well, I hope so," I muttered. I could feel myself

going red. How wonderful that James thought highly of me. I felt like I was walking on air.

India Hammond was in the collecting ring on the Dweeb and talking to a girl with glasses on a piebald pony. Bean and Dee-Dee went to help adjust poles for James and Moth to practice over, and as James's mom and I stood anxiously waiting for James to jump, I could hear the Dweeb and the piebald pony talking.

"How's it goin'?" the piebald asked in a drawl. I remembered that I had promised myself to do some research into whether ponies had regional accents—and this seemed to confirm it.

"Well, I find this all a bit—forgive me—provincial," said the Dweeb. She sounded really upper-crust and a bit conceited.

"Whaddya mean?" said the piebald, not posh at all.

"Oh, you know, it's not quite what I'm used to. I mean, when one has jumped at the National Show Jumping Championship, coming in and competing against these ponies doesn't seem fair—for them, I mean."

"Oh, a bit beneath you, is it?"

"Quite! If I don't get a clear here, I might as well retire! Of course, the championship was in my younger days, and I'm not sure India even knows how good I really am. I changed homes so many times—as talented ponies do, you know. My name was Platinum Bell then. Ahh, wonderful times." She sighed.

"That must be a pretty big burden for ya," the piebald said sarcastically.

You know when you hear a snippet of information you know to be important, but you can't really unravel its significance at the time? I got that feeling when I heard the Dweeb, so I filed it away for future reference. I couldn't do much else right then because James and Moth galloped into the ring, grabbing all my attention.

"Oh, come on, James," breathed his mom, crossing her fingers on both hands. Bean and Dee-Dee scooted up behind us, and we all held our collective breaths. Moth looked fired up and ready for action. The pair of them flew around like they were late for an appointment—which is how Moth always tackles jumps—and only one flimsy pole dropped on a nasty upright, giving her a ten-second penalty. We all leaped in the air and screamed, "Well done, James!"

We grinned at one another. The ponies were being so great this time!

We followed James and a puffing Moth back to the tree and gave Katy the great news.

"Fantastic!" she cried. Then her face dropped. "Oh, I hope I'm not going to spoil it all."

"Don't be silly," I told her. "Bluey is our anchor pony!" It really did seem that we were invincible this time. We could easily drop Bean's score and still do well at this rate. I couldn't wait to see Catriona's face when she found out how improved we were.

We had at least half an hour before Bluey was scheduled to go cross-country, and it was when I was munching on yet another of James's mom's sausage rolls that my thoughts returned to what I'd overheard the Dweeb tell the piebald. Because I thought I remembered reading in the rules that this competition was restricted to ponies who were not at the national level. It was strictly not allowed to have any team members who had jumped under USEF rules. If the Dweeb had indeed been to the championship, then she wasn't eligible to compete in the Sublime Equine Challenge. My mind rambled on and reached an inevitable conclusion: the Dweeb's experience meant that Cat and Leanne's team was breaking the rules.

Cheating.

But then, just as that nasty word popped into my head, another worse thought followed it—was I cheating, too? Because there was no doubt about it, Epona had allowed me to listen to the ponies on my team, and it had dramatically improved our performance. If I hadn't heard them, would we still be struggling?

My head hurt.

I had to share this.

As Katy rode off on Bluey (with Bluey getting excited at the prospect of doing his favorite thing), I grabbed James and Bean.

"I've got something to tell you both," I told them. "I need your opinions."

"OK, let's have it," said James, between bites of an éclair. Cream oozed out and dripped onto his blue tie. I ignored it.

"You know the Dweeb?" I said.

"India's pony," said Bean, on the ball for once.

"Well, according to the rules, I think she's overqualified to be in this event."

James gave a low whistle. More cream spluttered out.

"Oh, puh-leeese!" wailed Bean, flicking bits of second-hand cream off her jacket.

"I overheard her saying she'd jumped at the national championship," I continued.

"So?" said Bean. I knew it wouldn't last.

"This competition is for ponies that have never competed under rules."

"The cheats!" Bean exclaimed, looking around wildly for the secretary's tent. "Let's tell on them, get them disqualified."

"Hold on…" I said, grabbing her arm. "I'm worried they might have something on us, too."

"Like what?" James said indignantly. "We're not cheating."

"No?"

"Get to the point, Pia!" Bean cried.

"Well, what about my little talk with the ponies? How can we explain our remarkable improvement? Cat and Leanne know about my Pony Whisperer status, they could complain about that, too!"

"Mmmm, tricky," said James, stroking his chin. Why do boys do that? "But they don't know about your chat with the ponies."

"They're cheating!" wailed Bean. "It's not fair!"

"I'm not sure they even know they're breaking the rules," I said.

"You're kidding!" exploded James. "How can they not know?"

"The Dweeb was called something else then. It was a long time ago. I don't think India is even aware of her history."

"Well, we still have to say something. We still have to get them eliminated," Bean said.

"They'll want to know how we know," murmured James.

"Exactly!" I said, thankful someone else appreciated the problem.

"Oh!" said Bean. Her forehead wrinkled as she worked it all out in her mind. Then, once she had, she shrugged her shoulders and sighed. "So we're stuck with it?"

"It looks that way," I said, thinking that things would have been simpler if I hadn't overheard the Dweeb's conversation. Epona wasn't always a blessing.

The loudspeaker announced the departure of Katy and Bluey as they galloped toward the first fence on the cross-country, and we watched as Bluey's black and gray speckled backside disappeared into the distance.

"God, wouldn't it be awful if Bluey made a mess of it," said Bean, chewing her nails.

"Shhh, don't say that!" I said.

Bluey didn't. He romped home after a fabulous round, and we all jumped up and down, hugging one another.

The Great Eight finished third behind the professional team of chestnuts and a team of three boys and a girl who looked like they'd been doing this all their lives. We were sooo excited—and a bit stunned!

"We'll have to get your mom to come along next time," said Bean. "She's our good-luck charm."

"And if she brings some more food, that'll be awesome!" I agreed.

"Yes, you greedy pigs," interrupted Katy. "I never did get any of that. Any left?"

"No chance!" James laughed.

We made a huge fuss over the ponies.

"Well, we kept our word," said Drummer.

"You were wonderful!" I told him, keeping ours. I hugged his neck, planting a huge kiss on his cheek.

"Awww, get off!" he mumbled.

"But do you realize the best part?" James said.

"What?" said Katy, rummaging around the cooler for crumbs.

"Team SLIC had a disastrous day—poor Warrior got bitten by a horsefly as he was doing his cross-country round and went ballistic, which meant Scott had to retire. That means we've each got one qualifier under our belts, and both teams need to finish in the first three next time to qualify. With any luck, if the next qualifier turns out like this one, we won't have to worry about the Dweeb's secret, after all!"

"What secret?" asked Katy.

"Oh, we'll fill you in on the way home," Bean said as we got ready to go to get our ribbons. As we rode over to the main ring I looked over to the horse trailer line. Leanne and Cat were staring at us, and they looked anything but happy. I pushed any negative thoughts to the back of my mind. I wanted to enjoy the feeling of success for a while longer, and we reveled in euphoria as we rode home. Even the ponies picked up the mood and were in high spirits. For me, it lasted until I got home.

CHAPTER 9

YOU SEE, IT WAS like this: Mom's nightmare friend Carol had dropped by and they were chatting up a storm. OK, so Mom asked me about how the challenge had gone. She made all the right "Oh, I'm delighted for you, Pia," noises for, like, five minutes, and then she swooped in with Greg updates and took it from there. Because she'd been out for the day with Greg.

They'd started at a coffee shop watching the street performers. Then they'd walked around the park and fed the squirrels. Then they'd had lunch somewhere really fancy, with wine and everything—even though my mom gets a bit sloppy when she's had a drink. Then Greg insisted they go to a museum to look at the weird art, only Mom said she couldn't get her head around it and Greg had lectured a lot. Mom giggled as she told us she'd spent five minutes nodding sagely at an exhibit before realizing it was a radiator (Carol screamed with laughter at this point). And then they'd caught the train home where, apparently, there was kissing. I so didn't want to go there—gross squared!

"I can't wait to meet him," said Carol, helping herself to a cookie. I couldn't wait for her to meet him either. I didn't think Carol would take to him at all. She liked them a little wilder than cotton-ball-hair Greg.

"He's so nice," raved Mom. "He complimented me on the dress I wore today—"

"Oooo, that's good. This one?" Carol interrupted, peering at Mom's dress.

"Yes, he said it was a nice change to see a woman wearing something feminine," Mom continued. "Greg said that he likes to see a woman in a dress."

Oh, did he? I thought.

"And he said it made a nice change to be seen with someone who takes pride in her appearance," said Mom, a bit smugly.

"Oh, not so good. It sounds like he's training you," said Carol, helping herself to another cookie. "That's typical talk for someone who wants to dissuade you from wearing pants."

I thought so, too. Greg sounded pretty creepy.

"Oh, Carol, you're reading too much into it!" Mom laughed.

"Did he say anything else?"

"Well, he wouldn't let me go halves with the lunch bill. And he said he liked my hair up, and that I should always wear it like that."

"See!" exploded Carol. "He is training you!"

"It was just a compliment!" Mom laughed.

"Just watch him," Carol said darkly, brushing crumbs off her ample chest. "He sounds manipulative to me."

And me, I thought, without saying anything. That was a first, Carol and me agreeing on something. Usually, she's the one egging Mom on and throwing caution to the wind. It seemed she had her doubts about Greg, and so did I. But then, I wondered, would I always have doubts about Mom's boyfriends, simply because they weren't my dad? I imagined the future with Greg and Mom as an item. Not attractive. I went to bed, leaving Mom and Carol giggling over a bottle of wine. Honestly!

The next day at the yard, James rounded up the human members of the Great Eight for a meeting in the tack room.

"What are we meeting about?" asked Bean, yawning.

"I just thought we ought to formulate our action plan for the next qualifier," James explained.

"Aren't we just trying our best to win?" said Bean. "Or is that too obvious?"

"OK, no need to be like that," said James.

"Sorry, but the farrier's due any minute, and I haven't got Tiff in from the field yet. You know what Dave's like if he has to wait around."

"Yeah, but he doesn't mind if he's late," said Katy. "I waited over two hours for him once, and he didn't even apologize when he finally turned up, *and* he spent another half an hour on his cell phone, booking in other people."

"Is he any good? Drummer's farrier keeps complaining about having to drive too far to shoe him. I might ask Dave to do him," I said.

"Can we concentrate on our action plan?" James interrupted. We all looked at him and remembered why we were there.

"Well, what do you suggest?" said Katy.

"How about we all watch one another as we practice and offer any advice? I mean, eyes on the ground are valuable, and we could really improve with some constructive criticism."

"I wouldn't like to comment on Bluey," I said, shaking my head. "As I see it, he and Katy are stars and don't need any help."

"I agree," said Bean, looking at her watch.

"Well, I could do with some help," said James.

"OK, we'll all watch you," said Bean, getting up to go. "Oh, no!" she exclaimed.

"What?" we all swiveled around to see.

"Twiddles-scissor-paws is sitting on my tack box. I can't get my halter."

"Are you going to let a fluffy little kitty cat stop you?" James grinned.

Twiddles is one of Mrs. Collins's cats. A fat tabby and a great mouser, he's all purry and nice-as-pie with Mrs. C, but morphs instantly into Demon Cat with everyone else. He scratches, he hisses, he doubles in sizes and fluffs up like a puffball cat if you so much as speak to him. Everyone's terrified of him, and if Twiddles chooses to sit on anything of yours, well, unlucky you is all I can say. Bean wasn't overreacting at seeing Twiddles all curled up and comfortable on her tack box.

"You chance it!" said Bean. "Katy, can I borrow your halter?"

"Yeah, of course," Katy agreed. "Come on, James, Pia and I will watch you jump Moth and make suggestions."

So Tiffany spent the next hour tied up in Bluey's purple halter having a pedicure, and Katy and I watched James take Moth around the jumps in the outdoor school. She thundered around, her hooves drumming on the sand surface, snorting through her nose in her usual dragon fashion. Only we didn't do much watching, as we were too busy jumping jumps and wings around, altering the height of poles and rearranging the course to James's liking. Moth was still taking the odd pole off with her hind legs—worryingly.

"You know what, Pia?" Katy puffed, struggling to push a jump cup through a hole in the wing. "We have so been set up."

"How?" I asked, hauling a pole around.

"Hey, James!" Katy shouted. "You just wanted us to alter the course for you, didn't you?"

James grinned. "No, I need your advice. Honest!" he yelled, aiming Moth for the double and leaning forward as Moth launched herself into the air. She really was an exuberant jumper.

"Oh, that's a dirty trick!" I yelled, dropping the pole in disgust.

"You're still helping. I can practice much more if I don't have to keep getting off to move stuff around. It's for the team!" James said cunningly.

"You ride with awfully long stirrups, James," observed Katy.

"Yeah, what of it?" James said, pulling up Moth for a breather.

"Well, I always shorten my stirrups at least two holes when I go cross-country," Katy said thoughtfully. "Perhaps your stirrup length is making Moth drop her hind legs too early. You're not able to stay off her back."

I looked at Katy, then at James. His stirrups were very long. Everyone knows you need shorter stirrups for jumping, but somehow this information had passed James by.

"I'll give it a try," said James, adjusting his stirrups there and then.

"Wow!" I exclaimed, as James and Moth cleared all the jumps in fine style. "It's like magic!"

"Yeah, well, we could use some magic to help us," said Katy. James caught my eye—little did Katy know that any success we'd had so far had relied heavily on some magic from a certain two-thousand-year-old stone artifact.

Epona!

CHAPTER 10

I'VE GOT IT!" CRIED Dee, handing out Popsicles. She'd stopped off at the convenience store on her way to the yard and bought one for everyone. Soon, all that could be heard in the tack room was the sound of slurping. It was a great idea because it was really, really hot. The tack room, however, was really, really cool, which made it the location of choice on a hot day.

"Got what?" said Bean, lifting her Popsicle up and out of reach of Mrs. Collins's greyhound, Squish, who had suddenly become everyone's friend.

"An idea on how we can make sure we qualify for Brookdale," Dee said.

"Well, don't keep it to yourself." I slurped.

"My granddad. He can help us."

Katy, Bean, and I looked at her blankly. James hadn't arrived yet, but he was due any moment as he had another jumping practice planned.

"Is he one of the dressage judges?" Bean asked hopefully, twirling her long blond hair up on top of her head to keep cool.

"No, he's dead."

We all stopped mid-slurp. We hadn't seen that one coming.

"Er, sorry, I'm missing something," said Katy. "Get lost, Squish, I don't hang around when you're eating your Kibbles 'n Bits!"

"We can call up his dear departed spirit."

"Oh, of course, we've been so stupid!" I said, slapping my forehead dramatically. "What are you on, Dee?"

"No, honest, it will work, I've done it before," she said earnestly. "We use an Ouija board and ask for his help. He used to be a whiz with horses when he was alive. Really good with them—rode at all the top shows. That's why my mom's so horsey. He died before I was born. He'll help us."

"You mom's horsey because your granddad died before you were born?" asked Bean, confused.

"No, because he was!" sighed Dee, like we were strange.

"He was what?" Katy asked.

"Horsey!"

"And you want us to call up his ghost?" Bean said slowly. For once, she wasn't the only one having trouble.

"Yes, of course!"

"And you've done it before?" Katy asked.

"Yes!"

"Gross!" exclaimed Bean.

"How can that help?" I said, finishing my Popsicle with a flourish and throwing the stick into the trash.

"I don't know, but I called him up with my cousin once, when she wanted help with her exams, and she passed with fantastic grades. Granddad helped her."

"How do you know?" said Katy.

"Because she was terrible at all her subjects."

At that moment, James arrived, and Dee gushed out her bizzaro plan again. But James was dead set on the Ouija board plan—and that wasn't supposed to be a joke.

"Great idea!" he enthused. "Is that Popsicle for me?"

It was, but when James tore open the wrapper, it had been morphed by the heat into creamy sludge and oozed out all over the floor, so Squish got lucky after all.

We decided that we had nothing to lose by giving Dee's idea a try, so an argument followed about what to use for an Ouija board. According to Dee, we needed to write all the letters of the alphabet on the board so that her grand-dad could spell out words of wisdom for us with a glass, which we would place, upside down, on the board. There was simply nothing around we could use. Then Katy had an idea.

"How about a tack box? We can draw letters on the bottom," she suggested.

Everyone had a tack box where they kept all sorts of stuff: grooming kit, treats, spare bandages. Katy's was big with purple hearts drawn all over it (who'd have guessed it?!), Bean's had a broken lock and was full of very old, very ratty, half-clean stuff (she's not very tidy). Pictures of Tiffany were stuck all over it, only they were curling up with the humidity, making the box look even more disreputable. Mine was painted white and I'd written DRUMMER across it. James had a filing cabinet his dad had thrown out, which was huge. Ironically, it had the least in it.

"Whose?" I said. I didn't fancy Dee's granddad going to work on the bottom of my tack box. Actually, I didn't like the whole idea much at all.

We all looked at one another. No one volunteered a tack box.

"I know," said James, taking a look down the drive to make sure there was no one about. "We'll borrow Mrs. Bradley's. She won't even know." Seizing Mrs. Bradley's small and compact tack box from under Henry's saddle rack, he flipped it upside down. You know those toy boxes that made a *moo*ing or *baa*ing sound when you turn them over? Mrs. B's tack box did a similar thing, only the sound it made was all her stuff tumbling from the bottom to the top. Anxious glances were exchanged.

"What makes you think she won't know?" said Bean, chewing her lip.

"Stop worrying!" said James breezily. "What do we do now, Dee?"

"You need to write the alphabet on it," said Dee, handing James the chalk from the blackboard where everyone left notes to one another like, "Katy, can you turn out Tiff on Tuesday, please, Bean." James wrote *A* through *Z* all around the box in a rather crammed circle. I pulled a face at Bean—I could tell by the way she wrinkled up her nose that she wasn't very excited about this idea either.

"Now we need a glass," Dee said.

"That's a no-no," said Katy. "Will this beaker do?"

"It will have to. Come on, we all have to sit around the board and put a finger on the glass—I mean beaker." Dee turned the beaker upside down and placed it in the center of the tack box.

"Close the door," hissed James, sitting down on an up-turned bucket. Katy shoved Squish out and pulled the tack room door shut. There wasn't much light—the window was full of cobwebs, but Dee said the gloom would give the spirits confidence to come to us. It didn't do my confidence any good. Then we all sat around the board and gingerly put our fingers on the beaker.

"Just lightly—don't press down too hard," instructed Dee. "Granddad's spirit goes inside the beaker and moves it around to spell out a message."

Bean snatched her hand back into her chest. "I really don't like this…" she said, shivering.

"Oh, Bean, don't be such a scaredy-cat," scoffed James, grabbing her hand and forcing her finger back onto the beaker. "Come on, Dee, call up Gramps!"

I didn't like this either, but not wanting to look like a wuss, I gingerly put my finger on the beaker and hoped nothing would happen. I hoped Mrs. Bradley wouldn't suddenly appear at the door, too. Try explaining that one, I thought. And I couldn't imagine Mrs. Collins being thrilled about us holding a séance in her tack room either.

"Is there anybody there?" Dee murmured, slowly and dramatically. Katy snorted, trying not to laugh.

"Shhh!" hissed Dee. "Is there anybody there?" she said over and over again. I started to relax. Nothing was happening—nothing was going to happen. I felt a bit stupid for feeling scared. Then, just as I was starting to get bored, the beaker moved.

"Ahhh!" screamed Bean, Katy, and I collectively, retracting our hands with lightning speed. The beaker went flying, and I could feel my heart thudding in my chest.

"Oh, you've ruined it—we were just getting somewhere!" wailed Dee.

"Come on, let's try again. And *don't overreact!*" instructed James sternly.

"You pulled back, too!" I pointed out.

"Yeah, well, I wasn't expecting it," James said, shrugging his shoulders.

Dee did her "Is there anybody there?" bit again, and the beaker moved again, to collective gasps.

"Who is it? Who is there?" asked Dee. The beaker started moving toward the letters, slowly at first, then faster.

"*A...d...a...m...r...*" spelled out Dee.

"James, you're moving it!" accused Katy.

"I am not!" hissed back James.

"Who is then?" whispered Katy.

"Shut up!" Dee hissed. "*O...w...e...*"

"Adam Rowe," said James. "He's moving it."

"Are you Adam Rowe?" said Dee.

"He just said he is," whimpered Bean.

"Or was!" said James dramatically.

"Is that your granddad?" I asked Dee. She shook her head. I felt a shiver run up and down my spine. I was liking this less and less by the minute. Who had we called up here?

"Do you have a message for us?" said Dee, completely unfazed.

"Ask him whether he can help us win the challenge," whispered Katy. "Or ask him whether he knows your granddad."

The beaker started moving around the board, spelling out a message.

"*B...a...d...d...e...a...t...h...b...a...d...d...e... a...t...*"

"I really don't like this!" moaned Bean, biting the nails on her free hand.

"Sorry to hear about your bad death," said James, rather irreverently. "But we have a pressing need to talk to Dee's granddad. Can you put him on, please?"

I gulped. This was totally getting out of hand. I mean, what if the bad death wasn't about the spirit we'd called up. What if...?

"We need help with the next stage of the Sublime Equine Challenge," said Dee, staying focused. "We need your help, Granddad. We know you had a special way with horses. Can you help us?"

The beaker stopped. Then it shuffled about and started on its journey again.

"*B...a...d...*"

"Oh, not again," grumbled James. The beaker stopped. Then started again.

"*H...a...v...e...f...a...i...t...h...*"

"Someone *is* pushing it. Who is it?" demanded Katy—only because she was whispering, she didn't sound very demanding. "OK, if that's really a spirit, prove it!" she continued.

"Oh, don't, you'll make it cross," wailed Bean, as the beaker went faster and faster in demented circles, not spelling anything at all.

"If you are a spirit, then make Squish bark!" challenged Katy, which was clever of her because Squish never barks.

Only at that precise moment, *he did*. No, really, he did, exactly then!

Not surprisingly, pandemonium broke out in the following order:

1. Everybody screamed.
2. After scrambling to our feet, we burst out of the tack room, pushing one another aside in our best disaster-movie impression.
3. Because of our undignified exit, Mrs. Bradley's tack box defied gravity and flew up toward the ceiling.
4. We were all out in the sunshine by the time the tack box hit the floor with an almighty crash.

Bean wailed like one of the cats, I couldn't stop myself from shuddering, and Katy was as white as a sheet. James was bent over double, he was laughing so much. Dee just looked cross.

"You ruined it!" she said to Katy.

"Me? What did I do?"

"Oooh, I never want to do that again!" groaned Bean, wrapping her arms around in a self hug. I agreed with her.

"That was so not a good idea, Dee!" I muttered.

Katy gave James a shove. "You were so pushing that beaker, James. I know it was you!" Whether she really thought so, or whether she wanted to believe it was James spelling out the words, we couldn't tell. I know I wanted to believe James was responsible.

"I couldn't make Squish bark, though, could I?" said James, grinning at her. I didn't want to think of that—it was just too creepy.

We sent James back in to return Mrs. Bradley's tack box to its rightful place. We were all too freaked to have anything more to do with it.

"So Granddad said to have faith," mused Dee, tapping her chin with her finger and looking thoughtful.

"Oh, Dee, you don't really think that was your granddad, do you?" I asked.

"Of course, I told you, he's helped out before. Just you wait and see!" she said, nodding. "Now Granddad's onboard, you'll breeze through the next qualifier. You just see if you don't!"

It wasn't until later when I was de-cobwebbing Drummer's stable from a distance with a broom (which takes me a long time, 'cause if I see a spider, I have to run out of the stable until it's gone), and my thoughts were rambling along like they do, when I wondered whether I could summon up the spirits to do something about Skinny Lynny. Like make her disappear. Or get tired of my dad, or diet away to nothing—or at the very least, never want to go riding again. Or could I influence my dad and get him back together with my mom? And if I could, would Mom want that? Would I?

And then my thoughts meandered on to considering whether I could make Greg less of a nerd, or even make him go away altogether. Perhaps he could join the navy or get lost on a school trip in the mountains. But just as I had Greg stuck down a hole in the Rocky Mountains, calling for help, with no one within earshot, a spider dropped down too close for comfort and forced me outside.

In the sun, I realized I was getting really carried away with this spirit stuff. How easy it is for evil to take hold, I thought. I really had to get a grip. Mom says it's seriously bad karma to wish ill on other people (she usually says it after a mega whining session about Skinny Lynny), and that it will only come back on you twofold. So then I got to wondering whether I would try the Ouija board thing out on Skinny and Greg if karma wasn't the only thing stopping me, and whether karma and conscience were the same thing, and in the end my head started to feel a bit full with so many thoughts so I took Drummer for a ride and let the dust settle in his stable and my brain.

When I got into bed that night, and started imagining all sorts of things—mainly when I heard a floorboard squeak or could hear all the usual night sounds, which seemed suddenly spooky—I totally wished we hadn't let Dee talk us into the Ouija board thing. I made up my mind I was never, ever going to do it again.

CHAPTER 11

THE THIRD QUALIFIER WAS make-or-break time. If we didn't place in the first three here, it was bye-bye, Brookdale dream. I couldn't help wondering whether Dee's granddad really was looking down on us. (Or up. I mean, how could we tell?)

It took us forever to ride over to Lambourne Farm, which is a really fancy equestrian center on top of a hill. It was a hot day, so we got there early so the ponies could rest before the competition. The dressage was held in the massive indoor school. Tiffany and Bean were up after a particularly good test by a gray pony ridden by a very tall girl who sniffed all the way around.

"Why doesn't she blow her nose?" hissed Bean.

"Perhaps it's a habit," I hissed back. "Can you remember the test?"

"Don't ask!" she said. "And don't put me under pressure, for goodness sake!"

Tiffany and Bean performed in their usual fashion—two missed transitions, one wobble when Bean was undecided about a circle or a turn, and one stop-dead-and-check-out-the-letters-before-proceeding-with-caution. Her score was thirty-nine. What could we say? Bean had warned us how it would be. Outside the arena, Tiffany rubbed her nose on a front leg to get rid of the feel of the noseband.

"You think it would get easier," she said to me. "But actually, it's worse each time."

"We all appreciate your bravery, Tiff," I told her, patting her snowy mane.

"Still trash, though. You all have to pull your hooves out," Tiff told Drummer and Moth. "I'm done for the day! I don't like the look of those flags, by the way. Very nasty."

Our ace in the hole, Bluey, completed his customary fast clear. He was like a machine. We sponged him down with some cool water as Katy slithered out of the saddle and thanked him. Scott and Warrior thundered around with no penalties whatsoever, and it looked like it would have taken a natural disaster to stop them or even slow them down.

"I wish we'd had a big fat horsefly on our side today." Bean sighed, obviously not the slightest bit worried by karma.

"We only have to come in third to qualify," James reminded us.

Drum gave his best performance yet ("The sooner it's over, the sooner I can get out of this ridiculous costume!" were his exact words) and we got a high score from the judges. I didn't see Cat and Bambi's performance as they had been the first to go. From the scoreboard, I could see they had a good score—better than mine.

"No pressure, James," remarked Bean. "But it's all up to you now!"

"Piece of cake!" said James. But he pulled a face to show he wasn't taking anything for granted. Since altering his stirrups, Moth had hardly touched a pole, and although he and Moth had a nasty moment at a tricky fence, and Moth slipped going into the style, causing us all to hold our breath, nothing fell, and we all leaped up and down and squealed like boy band fans when James rode out with a clear round and no penalties. The Great Eight were on their way up!

"See," said Dee, "I said my granddad would help us."

"I don't see why he should take all the credit," said James.

"He didn't help me much," grumbled Bean. "It took me ages to get to sleep that night. I kept imagining all sorts of things whenever I heard a squeak or a thump. It was a lousy idea."

I was glad I hadn't been the only one who'd imagined things when I'd gone to bed. I didn't think it worth mentioning.

India was next to jump on the Dweeb. As she cantered into the ring, we had a bit of a powwow.

"Is that the pony who's overqualified?" Katy whispered to me.

"Yes. She was called Platinum Bell when she jumped at nationals."

"It doesn't make sense," said Dee. "Well-known ponies command a higher price, so why would anyone want to keep it a secret? I can't believe India doesn't know her pony is so experienced."

"Maybe there's a reason for it," suggested Bean. The

bell rang, and India headed the Dweeb, aka Platinum Bell, toward the first jump.

"What kind of reason?" I said.

"I don't know. Perhaps India stole her," Bean suggested wildly.

India and the Dweeb cleared the first jump and cantered neatly toward the next. I couldn't get the image of India, in cartoon-burglar garb of a black-and-white striped top and black mask, unbolting the Dweeb's stable and leading her away in the dead of night. No, that couldn't be it.

"Or," said James, "perhaps she just likes winning at local shows on a pony who can blow the opposition away."

Tucking up her forelegs neatly, the Dweeb cleared the style with plenty of room to spare.

I looked at James. "Are you serious?"

"I don't know." He shrugged. "I'm just clutching at straws. India doesn't seem the sort to pull a fast one. She's actually pretty nice."

Twang went my heart. James thought India was nice.

"I know," agreed Katy. "I can't believe she knows about her pony's past."

The pony who had told the piebald that she thought these qualifiers were a bit "provincial" got it all wrong at the next and dropped her hind legs onto the pole, knocking it off and collecting ten penalties.

"Hooray!" yelled Bean, immediately clapping her hand over her mouth and turning bright red. "Oh, dear, I so didn't mean to say that out loud. Sorry."

Several people nearby tut-tutted, so we crept away, trying to look ashamed.

A team of two chestnuts, an Appaloosa, and a bay won the qualifier, ridden by three sisters and their cousin. They had a big horse trailer and looked very serious about it all. Cat and Leanne's team was second, and we went wild when the loudspeaker announced that the Great Eight had taken third place.

Two-thirds. We'd qualified!

"I don't believe it—we're going to Brookdale!" shouted Katy, hanging around Bluey's neck and smothering him with kisses. Bluey looked pleased in a pleased-pony sort of way.

Bean did a dance on the spot, causing Tiffany to stick her head in the air and run backward.

"Hear that, Moth? We're off to the big-time!" James said. Moth said nothing.

"Drummer, you're going to Brookdale, what do you think of that?" I told Drum.

"Do I have to wear those ear things there?" Drum replied.

"Oh, I so wish I was on the team. It's not fair!" wailed Dee.

"But you're always riding Dolly at all the top shows!" Katy reminded her.

"It's not the same—really, it isn't," Dee whined.

I couldn't believe we were going. We really were going. To Brookdale.

I imagined riding around the famous arena, bumping into show jumpers, being applauded in the main ring. Awesome!

We hastily straightened ourselves up so we wouldn't

look too shabby next to the horse trailer–sister–cousin combo, and we were excitedly waiting to go into the main arena to collect our ribbons when the loudspeaker crackled into action again, informing everyone that an objection had been lodged. And that it needed to be cleared before the placings could be recorded. It boomed out across the showground to tell everyone that the objection was against a member of the Great Eight.

Pia Edwards.

Me.

CHAPTER 12

GULPED. WHAT HAD I done? Had I broken the rules? If so, how? Which bit of equipment had I left off Drum? Thoughts raced around my head, but I couldn't imagine what the objection could be about.

"It's your awful granddad," Bean hissed to Dee. "I bet it's against the rules to get help from dead relations."

"Who would know?" mumbled Dee guiltily.

"You should let dead granddads lie," Katy told her.

"What could be the reason, Pia?" James asked, and I shook my head and shrugged my shoulders. How could I know?

"I'll come with you. Let's go," he said grimly, and leaving Drum and Moth with the others, we made our way to the secretary's tent. And guess who was there with two of the organizers—a woman in glasses and a man in a tweed coat? Cat and Leanne. My heart sank. If Cat was behind this, it had to be bad. James said who we were, and the woman looked all flustered at me over her glasses.

"I'm Julia Williams and this is Robert Best. We're two of the judges for this Sublime Equine Challenge." We knew that. They both wore name badges under another enamel badge that said JUDGE.

"What seems to be the problem?" James asked briskly. My throat seemed to have dried up, and I didn't trust myself to speak. I felt guilty, even though I was sure I hadn't done anything wrong.

Julia Williams turned to Cat. "Er, well, this young lady seems to think your teammate has an unfair advantage," she explained.

"You know what I'm talking about," cried Cat, lifting her chin defiantly. Leanne looked a bit uncomfortable.

"No, I don't," I croaked. Because I didn't.

"You're a Pony Whisperer. You can communicate with the ponies. That's how you do your wild card show. It isn't fair, and you know it!"

I sniggered. I couldn't help it.

"It's no laughing matter, young lady," said Robert Best sternly.

"It is!" I said, turning to Cat. "You've always said I wasn't a Pony Whisperer! You've always insisted that I was lying. But now that it suits you, you want me to be." I could feel Epona in my jodhpurs pocket, and a shiver ran down my spine. They couldn't search me, could they?

"That is true, Cat," James said. Then he turned to Robert Best. "Honestly, Mr. Best, Ms. Williams, do you really believe that Pia here can possibly communicate with ponies? I mean, do you?" He was a cool one; James knew that I could.

Both judges looked sheepish. Clearly, they didn't believe it at all. Julia Williams coughed. "Well, we have to take all objections seriously," she said, "and Catriona here says that Pia has been on the television, with her own show."

My heart did a somersault. She had me there, I couldn't deny that. Was I going to be disqualified? If so, our team would be out, with no chance of getting to Brookdale. Cat was just being spiteful—she'd qualified for Brookdale, and getting me disqualified didn't benefit her or her team at all. I couldn't understand why she was being so mean. The trouble was, Cat was right—I did have an advantage, a huge one. But then, I realized with a start, so did she. Glancing at James, I could see that the same thought had occurred to him, too.

"Hey, Leanne," he said. "Got a minute? Outside?"

"What? Now?"

"Oh, yes, right now! Excuse us." James steered Leanne out of the tent.

"Now, Catriona," said Julia Williams, "how can you possibly prove your incredible accusation?"

"Yes, Cat, how are you going to do that? Ask the ponies?" I said sarcastically.

"You're a cheat!" Cat said quietly, her green eyes blazing.

"Well, I really don't see how we can reach any kind of agreement on this," said Julia Williams.

"But the fact remains that an objection has been lodged," interrupted Robert Best. "If this girl has had her own television show, then we have to believe that she has some ability and may, with all things considered, have some advantage..."

Things were looking grim. Where was James? What was he doing? And why was it taking him so long?

"Therefore, I have no choice but to uphold—"

"*Stop!*" shouted Leanne, bursting into the tent with James hot on her heels. "We've changed our minds. We don't want to lodge an objection after all."

"*What?!*" screamed Cat, totally losing it.

"Yes, I mean, no, I mean, we honestly don't want to. Sorry, but it's all been a terrible mistake. Come on, Cat, let's go."

"But she's about to be thrown out!" Leanne whispered something in Catriona's ear. Cat said nothing. She just pressed her lips together, turned white, and stormed out of the tent with Leanne running to catch up with her.

"That seems to be the end of the objection," said James meekly, smiling at Julia Williams and Robert Best.

"This is all very irregular," said Robert Best.

"Well, I'm glad it's all resolved." Julia Williams sighed, clearly not a fan of confrontation.

Relieved, we bolted back to the others and got them up to speed.

"Good thing we had an ace up our sleeves," explained James. "If Pia hadn't overhead the Dweeb fessing up to the piebald, we'd have been out for sure. It was a close one."

"But that just makes it worse," said Katy, who is very honest. "It was Pia's pony whispering skills that allowed her to find that out in the first place, proving Cat's point. Maybe we should be disqualified."

"Oh, Katy, don't be so noble!" exclaimed Bean. "Cat's team has a red-hot show jumping pony to help them. That's cheating, too. Even more so!"

"But now they go through, too," Dee pointed out. "That can't be right either!"

"Well, we'll just have to beat them fair and square at Brookdale!" said James.

I shuddered. It had been a narrow escape, and I felt a bit shivery about it. Technically, Cat was right, I did have an advantage, a big one. But they had championship show jumper Platinum Bell on their team. If either team won the Sublime Equine Challenge, would that be right? How could we justify two wrongs—when everyone knows they don't make a right.

Whether it was wrong or right, I couldn't let the team down now. I twirled Epona around in my pocket. Ever since I'd found her, she'd presented me with problems—this was just her latest. But I was in this thing now, and in too far to stop. James was right; we had to beat Catriona's team fair and square. But could we? And if we did, weren't we just as bad?

Why were things always so difficult? Oh, pooh, pooh, pooh!

CHAPTER 13

DESPITE THE BAD FEELING with Leanne and Cat, I was really excited about Drummer and me going to Brookdale. I mean, how totally fab was that? I kept grinning to myself and jumping up and punching the air and shouting "*Yes!*" to no one at all. I couldn't wait to tell Mom all about it. But when I got home, there was a note in the kitchen to say she'd gone to some classical concert with Greg, and that she'd left me a chicken pot pie in the fridge. Mom always said she hated classical music, said it put her in a bad mood. She always preferred modern music. She even liked some rap. I wondered whether she'd told Greg about that. It seemed Carol was right—Greg was training my mom, and music was the latest subject.

A vision of life with Greg wafted before my eyes: Greg taking up valuable space on our sofa, feet up, eyes shut, hands conducting a violin concerto. Greg in charge of the TV remote, forcing us to watch cultural programs instead of the usual mindless stuff we like, and asking us questions all the way through to check whether we were paying attention. Greg going on about collective nouns and personal pronouns and being all teacherish—*all the time!* It was too unbearable for words. As I banged a plate onto the countertop and slammed the cutlery draw shut, the séance idea never seemed so appealing.

Then my cell phone rang. It was Dad.

"Hi, Pumpkin!" he boomed down the phone. He was always so happy these days, and I realized with a pang that I couldn't remember him being like that when he'd been with us.

"Hello, Dad," I replied, glad I could tell him about Brookdale. I was dying to tell somebody! I'd worry about the "pumpkin" thing another day.

"Oh, that's marvelous, Pia," enthused Dad, after I'd explained. "I'm very proud of you. When is it? We'll have to come and see you, especially as Lyn is having riding lessons at Stocks Hall. Her instructor says she's a natural."

What?! A green film of jealousy misted over my eyes. What I wouldn't do to have lessons at Stocks Hall—I'd ride like an Olympic gold medalist if I did! There could only be three reasons why Skinny's instructor said she was a natural:

1. The instructor was either a. blind or b. stupid (or both!).

2. He was sucking up 'cause lessons at Stocks Hall cost an arm and a leg.

3. Skinny was, indeed, a natural.

Obviously, it had to be one of the first two—or possibly both.

"You'll have to go riding together," Dad went on. "How about on vacation? We could go to Greece, or Spain, or a

117

riding safari in Africa. I might even try riding myself! A vacation together would be fun, wouldn't it, Pia?"

I decided not to go there. My brain was hijacked by the image of the Ouija board again. I had to get a grip and put that out of my mind—talk about evil taking hold!

Dad rattled on some more, telling me all about how he and Skinny had been there, done that, blah, blah, and I said "oh, nice" and "really?" and "sounds good" in all the right places, and then he hung up after reminding me of his plan for us all to go riding together. He was certainly on a mission there.

He didn't ask about Mom. He used to in the early days when he left her for Skinny, but now he didn't seem to care. I heard myself sigh. Maybe an African safari would be cool. I wondered what the horses would be like in the bush, and whether Epona would let me hear what the zebras were saying.

The smell of burning pastry snapped me out of my thoughts, and I turned off the oven, feeling a bit sorry for myself. Dad hadn't got the relevance of my Brookdale news at all. I wanted someone to get excited with me, to scream and be all animated and tell me what a terrific, thrilling, amazing thing I'd done and how clever I'd been. I mean, that's what parents are for, aren't they? To build you up? Not run on about their girlfriends or leave you with a chicken pot pie for company while they go and listen to Schubert or Chopin or whatever. Right now, I wanted it to be about me. Me, me, me!

Mom still wasn't home by the time I went to bed, so she still didn't know her daughter's huge, amazing news. I went to bed really annoyed—which seemed very wrong seeing as I'd qualified to go to Brookdale, if anyone was interested. Which they clearly were *not!*

The next day, I decided to sulk and keep my Brookdale news to myself. Mom, however, couldn't wait to tell me all about her evening.

"But you always said you hated classical music," I muttered, determined to remind her.

"Yes, I know, Pia, but I need to keep an open mind. New experiences are so broadening. Greg says I need to go places I wouldn't think of going to, to open my mind to new experiences. He says I really ought to learn to appreciate the arts."

"Not if you don't enjoy them," I said, determined to disagree with everything Greg said.

"But Greg says I don't know whether I'll enjoy them. I need to discover that there's a whole world out there."

"OK, does that include asking whether other people have exciting news?" I hinted.

"I need to go shopping," Mom said, ignoring me. "I'll ask Carol to come with me. I need some new clothes, something more suitable for classy events. Everyone there last night was more dressed up than me. Greg says I need something long, an evening dress. I'm letting him down."

"Did he actually say that?" I said, feeling my hackles rising.

"Well, not in so many words, but I did feel kinda frumpy,"

she continued. "I could tell Greg was uncomfortable—embarrassed even, especially when we bumped into some friends of his. They all looked very elegant. Perhaps I'll try that fancy boutique in town...what's it called...Toto...Totum...Too-too?"

"The one you said was run by the old bag with the face-lift?" I reminded her. "Who sells the sort of clothes you always said were over-the-top and overpriced?" I went on, rubbing it in. Honestly, what had Cotton-Ball-Hair done to my mom?

"Well, I need something. I don't want to feel like that again. Greg's taking me to an exhibition at Splash! that fancy art gallery next week, and he said I'll need to dress up. But I'm not sure I can carry off anything too couture. I'm still carrying some extra weight. Greg says I need to loose at least five pounds, and—"

"*What?*" I screamed.

Mom stopped and looked at me as though she'd just remembered I was there.

"Listen to yourself!" I ranted. "Greg says this, Greg wants that, Greg thinks something else. What do you want, Mom? Do you really want to be with a man who makes you feel shabby? Who tells you you're fat? Who tells you what to wear? Shouldn't you be with someone who likes you because of what you are now, not what he wants to make you into?"

Mom looked stunned, but I was off, and I couldn't stop now.

"You were fine when you met Greg, now all you do

is what he wants. Remember how you were when Dad left? You're ten times more confident now. You don't need Greg—or anyone like him. You need someone who accepts and appreciates you for yourself. Who does Greg think he is, anyway? He's so nerdy, Mom, he doesn't deserve you."

"That's enough, Pia!" Mom found her voice at last, and I realized how rude I'd been. But I'd had it up to here with Greg. My mom didn't need him. Couldn't she see it?

"I'm going to see Drummer!" I yelled, running out of the door and slamming it behind me. I was behaving badly, but I was really upset at the thought of Greg telling my mom what to do—and he'd completely overshadowed my news of qualifying for Brookdale!

By the time I got to the yard, I felt dreadful. I hate fighting with Mom. Close to tears, I found Drummer in the field, rubbing his tail on a tree.

"Hey," I said crossly, "stop that!"

"I think I've got pinworms," he grumbled.

"So not the greeting I was hoping for!"

"Well, I thought you would want to know, so you can do something about it," he said. "You're sweetness and light this morning. What's up?"

"Family!" I said. "Oooh, they're so annoying!"

"Skinny Lynny?" asked Drummer.

"Not this time. It's Mom. Or rather, it's her latest boyfriend. He's such a know-it-all and he keeps bossing her around. I can't seem to make her see what a total loser he is."

"Mmmm, love is blind," Drummer said, his gaze drifting toward Bambi, who was rolling in the dust patch by the gate.

"Are you still infatuated with her?" I asked him.

"What can I say? She's the one." He sighed.

"She hates you," I reminded him.

"We're destined to be together. Bambi just doesn't know it yet. Besides"—he looked at me again—"people and ponies have to make their own mistakes. You can't stop them from taking wrong paths. It just makes them more determined to prove you wrong."

I don't know how Drummer knows so much about life and love and the universe and everything. Either he's very wise or he's just good at talking horse poop, which sounds more likely. I chewed the inside of my mouth and thought about it.

"But Greg's such a dork!" I wailed.

"Yeah, well, if that's true, your mom will see it eventually," Drum assured me. "Now, how about taking me in for a bite to eat? Something tasty, some pony cubes, maybe some sugar beet, a few handfuls of coarse mix? It must be breakfast time—and if we don't get a move on, it will merge into lunchtime, and I'll miss out. Come on!"

So we wandered in, and then Bean and Katy arrived, and we spent the morning practicing braiding manes and tails and dreaming about winning Brookdale and galloping around the big arena, and although Mom was still seeing Greg, and Skinny was still having riding lessons at Stocks

Hall, and nobody seemed impressed that I was going to Brookdale, it somehow didn't seem so bad when I was with everyone else and I had Drummer to talk to. It didn't seem so bad at all.

CHAPTER 14

IT WAS JAMES WHO thought of it. It was such a totally obvious thing to consider.

But nobody had.

Katy and I were doing the supportive thing for Bean, who was practicing her dressage schooling in the outdoor school, when James walked over to join us, his lips grimly pressed together.

"What's up?" I asked him.

"Oooh, is it gossip?" Katy cried eagerly, jumping down from the fence.

"Where am I supposed to canter?!" yelled Bean.

"Oh, let's see…" I looked at the dressage test sheet in my hand. "Canter a fifty-foot circle…at…A."

"What are you doing?" asked James.

"Bean's learning her final dressage test," Katy told him.

"But she's not supposed to practice the actual test." James sighed, like we had pony poop for brains. "If the judge thinks the pony's anticipating the next movement, she'll lose marks."

"Shhh!" I hissed, shaking his sleeve. "You know that, and we know that, but Bean's in such a state about remembering the test, she has to do it this way."

"Don't you say anything, James," warned Katy, putting

on her menacing face. "Just let Bean do what's right for her. We'll probably have to drop her score, anyway, so what does it matter? Get on with what you came to tell us."

James took a deep breath. "Has anyone given any thought as to how we are going to get to the final at Brookdale?" he asked.

"But we've qualified," Katy said in a voice that suggested James was being dim. "We're G-O-I-N-G!" She did a jig on the spot in glee.

"Yes, but how? How, physically, are we G-O-I-N-G? Ride all the way?"

"Oh," I said again, feeling as though someone had let the air out of my lungs. Obviously we did have pony poop for brains, otherwise we'd have thought of that. Brookdale wasn't a rideable distance.

"Mmmm, bit of an oversight, wouldn't you say?" agreed James, running a hand through his slightly-too-long blond hair. It has a peculiar effect on me, him doing that, but I couldn't dwell on that now.

"What's going on?" said Bean, pulling up next to us. Tiffany snorted dramatically at a snake in the sand before it turned back into a stick. We explained the crisis.

"Well, Katy's got a trailer. Two of us can go in that," said Bean, being a bit free and easy with Katy's trailer. But Katy nodded in agreement.

"But what about Moth and Drummer?" asked James. "Katy's dad can't make two trips, and Brookdale is miles and miles and *miles* away!"

I felt my spirits dribbling out of my boots and sinking into the grass.

"We'll just have to hire a horse trailer," said Bean matter-of-factly.

"But that will cost a *lot*," I said, chewing my lip. Mom and I weren't even going on vacation this year, so I knew we didn't have any spare cash for a horse trailer rental. The entry fees for the Sublime Equine Challenge had been difficult enough to scrape together, and I hadn't any pocket money left after forking out for Drummer's ear protectors and bells. James's family was obviously loaded, and I could only imagine how he was going to feel when I had to let him down. But James surprised me.

"I don't think my parents will pay for me to go," he whined. "They're helping my sister buy an apartment. They've made it clear that I have to fund any shows and events I want to do with Moth this year from my allowance."

We all stood around in gloomy silence. Tiffany rubbed her nose on the fence. Katy screwed up her face, deep in thought. I could almost feel the wind whistling through my head—empty of any ideas, as usual.

"I'm going for a ride," Bean announced in a wobbly voice, obviously totally let down. She rode off through the yard, her blond braid bobbing up and down, riding out a wobble halfway along the drive as Tiffany spotted a couple of monster rabbits. I couldn't be sure Bean wasn't actually crying, but I knew how she felt. It seemed so unfair that after everyone's hard work we weren't going to be able to get ourselves to the final. James, Katy, and I flung ourselves down on the grass in gloom.

"We should so have thought of this," James said.

"I can't believe we've been so stupid!" I agreed, angrily wrenching the head off a daisy.

We sat wallowing in misery, trying to think up ways to get around it and failing. When Dee arrived, declaring that she had some bad news of her own, we were less than sympathetic.

"I bet it's not as bad as ours," mumbled Katy.

"You're always complaining," said James, disappointment making him unkind.

"Yes, well, it's all right for you," wailed Dee. "You can do what you like up here. You should have your mom around all the time, telling you what to do with Moth, see how you like it."

"OK, Dee, what's your bad news?" said Katy, soothingly, anxious to avoid a scene.

"It's about Brookdale…"

"Yeah, ditto!" I said.

"I can't groom for the team at the finals—"

"No problem, actually," interrupted Katy, testily, "because the team can't go."

"*What?!*"

"It's true." I sighed. "Half of us can't get there because—"

"The transportation's too expensive," finished James, stealing the punch line. "Only two of us can go in Katy's trailer, so it's all been for nothing. So you see," he went on, "it's actually all right for you, for once."

You'll never guess what Dee did. You won't, so I'll have to tell you.

She *laughed!*

We all stared at her. I thought Katy was going to burst. James looked ready to do murder.

Dee stopped laughing and rolled her eyes skyward. "The other two can come with us," she said, like we were stupid not to have thought of it.

I felt my jaw dropping.

"Say again?" Katy said slowly.

"Yeah, we're going. That's why I can't groom for you. Mom's entered me and Dolly for a showing class there— it's a HOYS qualifier—and it's on the same day as the challenge. Our horse trailer takes four horses, and we're only taking Dolly, so there will be plenty of room. I'll ask Mom now, if you like." She poked her tongue out at James. James just looked flabbergasted. I'd never seen him lost for words.

I looked over to Sophie's huge and expensive horse trailer parked next to the barn. Could we really, possibly, ever in a million years, travel to Brookdale in that? We'd not just get there, we'd get there in style!

Dee's mom, Sophie, was completely supportive.

"Of course you must come with us," she gushed. "You've all done so well to qualify, and we're going anyway," she said in her usual, bossy tone. Which everyone forgave because she was being so generous.

So it was settled, and when Bean returned, after much

whooping and jumping about, we all had a powwow, and Bean and I biked to the village shop to get a box of chocolates for Sophie and a couple of bags of Whoppers and Marshmallows for us to celebrate. We all sat and had a major, delirious scarf-fest until Bean actually turned a bit green, jumped to her feet, ran across the yard, and disappeared. We just thought she was being strange as usual, but when she wobbled back she confessed to having thrown up a load of brown and pink goo on the muck heap—which we put down to the emotional roller coaster of the day. James felt the need to point out that it was a terrible waste of good Whoppers and Marshmallows. But then, I thought, that was far, far better than not being able to go to Brookdale, and we all (except Bean, who shook her head and rolled her eyes at the thought) sucked another Marshmallow each to that!

CHAPTER 15

"I CAN'T BELIEVE WE'RE REALLY here!" murmured Katy, looking around the famous Brookdale showground. The rest of the Great Eight nodded in agreement. It was totally awe-inspiring, competing at the same show as some of the most famous riders in the world. I could feel butterflies doing the rumba around my stomach.

We'd hit the road at six o'clock that morning. Bluey and Tiffany cocooned in Katy's trailer—Bluey swathed in purple from poll guard to boots, Tiffany in a more sophisticated two-tone blue ensemble. Drummer and Moth had been draped in their green (it's so Drum's color!) and black blankets respectively, and ready to go in Sophie's luxury horse trailer. Boy was it nice! With a ramp at the side and another at the back, four stalls, and living accommodations, Drummer had never traveled in such four-star luxury, and neither had I. I was almost as excited about traveling in that as I was about our destination.

Dolly had gone up the ramp first, and it immediately became clear why Dee hated going to shows with her mom.

"Tie her up a bit shorter," Sophie had barked from the bottom of the ramp. "Oh, come on, Dee, you've done it enough times!"

"Last time, you said I tied her too short!" Dee had protested.

"Sometimes, I think you do it deliberately, just to annoy me!" her mom had retorted, shaking her head.

"Why doesn't she do it herself?" I'd whispered to Dee when she came back down the ramp.

"Then she wouldn't have anything to complain about," Dee had whispered back. "She's always worse on show days—nerves."

With trepidation, and hoping I wouldn't get yelled at, I'd led Drummer up the ramp and tied him next to Dolly. Dolly had been made up.

"Oooh, hello, handsome. How lovely we get some quality time together at last!" she'd cooed as Drummer had sighed. Dolly's attentions embarrass him. I keep asking him why he doesn't just roll over and go for the glam Dolly, who clearly adores him, instead of rough old Bambi, but he says that love's like that. He must like a challenge.

"Can't Moth go here?" Drum had whispered out of the corner of his mouth. I'd grinned and patted his neck.

"Sorry! We don't get to choose. Sophie's in charge."

"Oh, I guess that's it then." Drummer knows an immovable force when he sees it.

With Moth safely loaded, and after a couple of minutes of Sophie berating Dee about loading tack and not forgetting this, and remembering that, and answering her cell phone a couple of times (she always seems to have her ear jammed to the phone, which is the only respite Dee gets),

131

Dee and Sophie got in the cab and James and I climbed into the living part behind them, and we'd set off down the drive after Katy's trailer.

To Brookdale. Did I mention that? I could so not sit still!

Twenty teams had qualified for the Sublime Equine Challenge—which meant that the showground was teeming with ponies, riders, and their supporters—and there were lots of the usual Brookdale showing and jumping classes going on at the same time. Having caught up with Katy's trailer on the way, Sophie parked her horse trailer next to it, so we were all together. I'd never seen so many fancy horse trailers in one place, and all that obvious wealth made me feel like a pauper. Katy's dad, who's all smiley and laid-back, settled down to read the paper, and Katy and James went off to find the secretary and get the lowdown on where everything was situated and the times we were due in which ring, leaving me and Bean to gaze all google-eyed at the exciting scene around us. It was a sunny day with a faint breeze, and the smell of hot dogs and doughnuts mingled satisfyingly with the smell of horses.

"I hope we see Ellen Whitaker," said Bean, her head on a swivel, trawling for horsey celebrities.

"Oh, look there's...em, who exactly is that?" I said as a man in show jumping gear whizzed past us on a bicycle.

"Dunno," said Bean, "but he must be someone famous. I thought I'd brought my autograph book..." she muttered, clutching her jacket pockets. The only thing I had in my pocket was a two-thousand-year-old goddess. Epona was safety pinned in to make sure she didn't go missing. What a disaster that would be!

"I wonder when my mom will get here?" I said, looking at the huge crowds. "Are your parents coming?"

Bean did a Tiffany-type snort. "You must be joking—they'd rather pull off their own heads. Let's go and look at the derby bank," she said, changing the subject and breaking into a run. I realized I'd never seen either of Bean's parents at the yard. What was the story there, I wondered. I realized that both my parents at least tried to take an interest in my interests. When I'd eventually told Mom about qualifying for the final, she'd been thrilled and totally excited.

The enormous derby bank looked like a huge, grassy, Egyptian pyramid.

"I can just imagine me and Tiff sliding down that," mumbled Bean, her mouth open in awe. Yeah, right, I thought. Tiffany would freak out half a mile away from it.

The main ring was vast, and all the jumps looked newly painted and familiar—the Devil's Dyke, the triple bar, the water jumps. I was in heaven knowing I wasn't just a spectator, but a competitor, just like my fave horsey celebs. My stomach did a sort of dance at the thought.

We wandered through the trade stands—we didn't have time to stop—and found our way back to the horses. We unloaded the ponies, stripping off rugs and travel boots and checking that they were OK. Moth had rubbed out one of her braids, so Bean fixed it before James and Katy returned.

"Here, I've got our numbers. Katy's got the times, and we walked the cross-country course together, so that's all done," said James, handing out the numbers.

"They've built the course especially for this event," said Katy, "and it's gorgeous. Bluey's going to love it!"

We looked at the note James held with our times written on it. James and Moth were up first, then me and Drum, followed by our secret weapon, Katy and Bluey (only they weren't much of a secret), with Bean and Tiffany going last. Seeing my name in the program prompted an excited tingle and a stab of fear. I wasn't the only one with worries.

"Oh, God, I'm last, and I just *know* I'm going to forget the test and let you all down," wailed Bean.

"You won't forget it this time," I said, crossing my fingers behind me against the probability of telling a big, fat lie. "You've practiced it so often at home, you'll remember it to-day." I didn't mean it. Secretly, I wished Katy was going last.

James wasn't so diplomatic. "We can drop your score, like we always do."

"Thanks for the vote of confidence!" yelled Bean.

"Oh, enough of the negativity!" snapped Katy, sticking her fingers in her ears. "No more what-ifs, puh-leeese! Unless it's to say, What if we all do fantastically well? What if we all perform like champions? What if we *win*? If you believe you'll do badly, you will. If you believe you'll do well, then guess what? You might just do that, instead!"

"Wow, that's telling us!" I said.

"OK, Katy, keep your hair on," mumbled James.

"If you say so," said Bean, unconvinced.

"OK, now give me five!" Katy said, sticking her arm in the air.

We did. Katy can be really scary at times.

Our supporters began to arrive. First were James's parents, and they'd brought Katy's mom with them. They all chatted with Katy's dad, said all the right encouraging things to us, then disappeared to have something to eat and go around the trade stands, promising they'd be watching all of us. There was no sign of my mom yet—or Greg, who was coming, too. I wondered whether he'd make me do detention if I didn't win. Or he might make my mom do it instead.

My dad and Skinny Lynny turned up though. But you'll never guess what Skinny was wearing. Jodhpurs! I could have died of embarrassment. Who wears riding clothes at a show when they're not competing? *She can't even ride!!!* I could see the others staring as Skinny stomped about in her leather boots and skintight jodhpurs and I could have died. Right there. Dead. At Brookdale. I imagined my teammates and Drummer shaking their heads as they gathered around me prostrate on the grass, saying, "It's sad, but going at Brookdale, well, it's what Pia would have wanted, after all."

"Hi, Pumpkin!" said Dad, kissing me out of my morbid thoughts and making me even angrier—with myself

135

this time. When was I going to have a word with him about that?

"When are you on?" asked Skinny, making an attempt to pat Drummer, then backing off as he flattened his ears back and swished his tail at her.

"Not until this afternoon. Why are you wearing jodhpurs?" I had to ask.

"Oh, I thought I'd blend in," Skinny replied airily, flicking back her hair.

"Don't they suit her?!" said Dad, giving her a dorky smile.

As one of my parents took his trophy girlfriend shopping at the trade stands, my other parent arrived with her boyfriend—the one with the glued-on hair.

"Hello, sweetie," said Mom, kissing my cheek. She was wearing a plain shirt and a pair of jeans over some flat boots, not very Greg-like at all. This merited investigation. As Greg admired Sophie's sensational horse trailer, I whispered to Mom.

"I thought you'd be wearing something unsuitable for a horse show, something Greg likes a woman to be seen in. What's going on?"

My mom turned a bit pink and faced me squarely. "I thought about what you said—about me doing what Greg wanted all the time. You were right. Greg was being manipulative. But I was to blame, too, for letting him influence me."

I was a bit stunned. "Oh," I said. Not the greatest of responses.

"So I decided that instead of running away from the

problem and simply finishing with him, I'd talk to him about it, put my point across."

"Oh," I said again. This was getting repetitive.

"He was actually really sympathetic to my feelings and what I told him. I was surprised," said Mom.

She wasn't the only one—I almost fell over. At least I didn't say "oh" again. I was starting to get on my own nerves.

"So we'll see how we go. At least I didn't cut and run. We're working through it instead of just running away from the problem."

My mom had stood up for herself. That was great.

It meant Greg was still ongoing. That was bad.

"That's fantastic, Mom," I heard myself saying. "I want you to be happy."

"Where's Drummer?" said Mom, as Greg came over.

I took them to where Drummer was tied to the trailer, munching on some hay. He was thrilled to see Mom. "Here's a woman who knows about the important things in life!" he said, frisking her for sweets.

Mom dished out the polo mints. Greg patted Drummer's nose.

"Who's the dweeb?" asked Drum, his minty breath wafting over us between crunches.

Mom wished me luck and assured me they'd both be watching us. Then, as it was time for James's jumping round, and we all got a bit frantic and twitchy, she and Greg disappeared and left us to it. I didn't have time to think any more about my Mom and her new way of dealing with things, but I was certainly going to give it some more thought later when I didn't have such a hectic schedule. I was shocked, amazed, and a little bit surprised.

CHAPTER 16

WE ALL HELPED JAMES saddle Moth, tweaking her brushing boots, straightening her noseband, and pushing James's tie right up to his shirt collar, then we followed them over to the show jumping ring. Everywhere was awash with Sublime Equine orange and lime banners, and the orange and lime dressed promo girls were there handing out catalogs and flicking back their hair. They looked just like Skinny Lynny. As all the dads ogled at them, the moms pulled disapproving faces and gave their husbands elbow nudges. Yup, just like Skinny, I thought with a sigh.

"The jumps look huge," gulped James, after walking the course and warming up over the practice fences. They did, but as Katy pointed out, in her official role of morale booster, that was because of all the fillers and flowers in them. They were, she assured James, no bigger than the ones he'd jumped at home.

James sidled up to me. "Can I borrow You-know-who for a quick confidence-building sesh?"

I screwed up my face. "Oh, James, I can't. She's pinned into my pocket with, like, a million safety pins, and it will take too long to get her out. Sorry."

James shortened his reins. "Well, we'll just have to do

it on our own, won't we, girl?" he said, patting Moth's chestnut neck.

Moth's bottom lip quivered, and she looked straight ahead, all wide-eyed as usual, her white face making her look really intense. If only she wasn't so nervous of everyone but James, I thought, stroking her neck. At least she's stopped flinching every time I touched her. That was progress.

"You can do it, Moth. We all believe in you," I whispered. And then the announcer was telling the crowd that the next to jump was James Beecham and Gypsy Moth, and Katy, Bean, and I held our breath and leaned on the fence as our first team members cantered into the ring.

"Oh, come on, James," said Katy, her fingers crossed.

The bell rang, and James and Moth raced through the start like they meant business, Moth's eyes opened wide at the fillers and flowers. They flew over the first four jumps at a blistering pace and in great style, and we allowed ourselves to breath out a little. Then there was a double, which Moth didn't like the look of—she snorted even more than usual, and James had to ride her strongly through, but nothing fell. A nasty, narrow gate was next, and although Moth's front hooves clipped it, it didn't fall (Bean put her hands over her eyes at this point, and I think I actually stopped breathing), and they then raced over a wall, a hedge, a couple of big spreads, and a water jump, before turning for the final three jumps, a nasty treble of shark's teeth.

"Come on…come on…" muttered Bean, jiggling up and down, riding Moth from the ground.

Moth took off too early over the first jump. Katy squeaked. Bean groaned and I dug my nails into my palms. Was this where our hopes fell apart?

The striding was all off for the second element, but Moth launched herself in the air and managed to clear it. But there was still the last jump to go. How could she do it? It looked impossible. Moth had no speed left, and the last jump was a spread, needing to be tackled from a strong pace. We watched as James legged on, urging his gallant chestnut mare on with his hands and heels. We heard him ask her for an extra effort with a desperate "*Hup!*" and saw Moth take off way, way too soon. Surely disaster was inevitable?

I couldn't look.

Screwing my eyes shut, I waited to hear the inevitable sounds of planks falling, the groan of the crowd, and the announcer shouting four faults. But instead, the longest ever silence was broken by the thud of hooves on grass, the crowd clapping, and the announcer shouting, "Clear round!"

"*Yes!*" shouted Bean, leaping up and punching the air.

"Oh, fantastic, Moth!" screamed Katy.

"But how?" I said astonished. "How?"

"She flicked her hind feet up over that last plank!" said Bean. "She's such a star!"

I'd missed Moth's Herculean effort by closing my eyes. I vowed never to be so wussy again.

Surrounding Moth as she came out, we all went bonkers and told them how clever they both were.

"It was all Moth!" James said, sliding out of the saddle and giving his mare a big hug. "She was just the best."

And Moth actually looked pleased with herself. Instead of her usual shrinking, don't-look-at-me demeanor, her eyes sparkled as if to say, "I did that. I pulled out all the stops and jumped my heart out for you all. I'm part of this team!" We each gave her a big kiss and a hug.

"What about me?" James laughed.

"We would if you were a horse!" Bean laughed, screwing up her nose and giving Moth another mint.

Talk about a missed opportunity!

CHAPTER 17

AWAITING OUR TURN IN the collecting ring, I swallowed hard. Drum and I really had to raise our game if we weren't to disgrace ourselves in front of everyone. And I had a score to settle with Cat—I just couldn't bear the thought of her beating me, not after she'd tried to get the Great Eight disqualified. My wimple wafted in front of my eyes, and I could hear a faint tinkle every time Drum shook his head against a fly.

A boy on a black pony was performing his routine. Dressed as a wizard, the boy rode his star-spangled pony in ever-decreasing circles to a Harry Potter sound track. Everyone around me murmured approval and nodded their heads. He seemed to be the favorite to win. I glanced around. Cat and Bambi had already performed their routine, and I could see them outside the collecting ring with Leanne and Scott. I watched as a woman joined them, a woman with a stroller and two young children. Lifting the bigger child, the woman gaily plopped her on Bambi's broad back, and I could see Cat looking less than happy about it. I was astonished—why was she putting up with it? She wasn't usually so accommodating!

"How did Cat and Bambi do?" I asked Katy, watching the child drumming its feet on Bambi's sides.

"Er, I can just see the scoreboard," said Katy, standing on tip-toe and screwing up her eyes. "Pretty well, she's in the lead at the moment. She must be thrilled."

"She doesn't look very thrilled," I said, my heart sinking. "Who's that woman over there with her?" I asked. "She just plonked her child on Bambi—and Cat doesn't look too happy about it. Why doesn't she tell her to get lost? I would if someone did that to my pony!"

"That's just the problem—" began Bean. "Ouch!"

I turned around and just caught Katy glaring at Bean, who was rubbing her elbow.

"What?" I said. "What's the problem? Who is she?"

"No idea," said Bean, a little too quickly. "Get ready, the wiz is almost done."

We were next—but I was determined to find out what Katy and Bean were hiding. There was some big secret about Cat and Bambi, something the others weren't telling me. They'd refused to tell me what it was all about before. I'm still the new girl, I thought with a pang.

The star-spangled black pony came out hot and puffing. Taking a deep breath I glanced over at James who was in charge of my music. He gave me the thumbs-up sign.

"Next to go is Pia Edwards and Drummer," announced the voice on the loudspeaker.

My mouth was dry, and I could feel my legs shaking. My hand went to my pocket where Epona was safely stashed away. We needed some magic now.

"Come on," cried Drummer, confidently, jingling as

he stepped forward. "Let's knock 'em dead!" His confidence rubbed off. It was now or never. Taking a deep breath, I stepped into the ring with him for our Brookdale debut—the stuff of dreams. Except that I didn't have the stars and stripes on my jacket and I wasn't jumping for my country. I was dressed in a yellow dress and my pony wore bells on his ears. It wasn't quite a fulfillment of my wild ambitions, but, hey, everyone has to start somewhere.

The ring seemed huge, and there were what looked like thousands of faces all turned in our direction. Strange then that Catriona's face loomed out of the crowd, forcing my confidence into my boots. But then our music started, and Drum was already into our routine. Tearing my gaze away from Catriona, I concentrated on the job at hand. I couldn't let Drum down now!

Drum was as good as his word—he was magnificent! He didn't just do the routine hoof-perfect, he jingled in all the right places, he tossed his head and gave exuberant leaps, he was just fantastic—talk about playing to the crowd! I remembered to smile and exaggerate my movements, and everyone loved us! They laughed in all the right places and clapped like crazy at the end. Except Cat, of course. She just stood outside the ring with her arms folded, looking sullen. Drum and I took a bow and skipped out of the ring where our teammates surrounded us.

"Awesome!" declared James, nodding his head.

"Oh, wow, well done, Drummer!" cried Katy, dishing out the mints.

"You were so the best, Pia, by miles!" said Bean, even though she hadn't seen any of the others.

"Better than the Harry Potter wannabe, anyway," mumbled James.

We waited for the score. It was out of twenty, and anything over fifteen was considered pretty good. When it was written on the scoreboard I almost fell over.

"Oh, Pia, you've got nineteen!" squealed Katy, dancing around in delight.

"You're *in the lead!*" screamed Bean, clutching my arm.

"Take that, Potter boy!" growled James.

I gave Drummer the biggest hug of his life. "You are the best pony in the whole world!" I told him, burying my face in his braided mane.

"Yeah, yeah, tell me something I don't know!" said my pony. For once, I decided his smugness was justified.

There was no time to linger. Drum, Katy, Bean, and I wandered back to the horse trailer where Dee was getting ready for her showing class. I hardly recognized her. She wore a beautiful blue velvet cap on top of her hair, which was wound into a tight bun. With a cream shirt, blue and scarlet spotted tie, navy jacket, soft brown leather gloves, cream jodhpurs, and brown boots, she looked a million miles from the scruffy Dee-Dee we were used to seeing at the yard.

"Wow, Dee, look at you!" exclaimed Bean.

"Yeah, I know, I look ridiculous." Dee sighed.

"You look fabulous!" I said.

Dee's mom didn't think so.

"Dee, your tie isn't tight enough, and your hat's on crooked. Come here and hold Dolly…there. Oh, for goodness sake, don't let her eat, she'll spit green slime all over herself. Must I do everything? Wake up! Stand still while I tie on your number. There. OK, leg up; one…two…no, are you doing this deliberately? On three, we always do it on three. Try again. One…two…three. Now ride her in over there—find a space—and get her on the bit and working properly. If she doesn't qualify for HOYS here, then we might as well give up and take up knitting. And *smile!* Hello, hello?" Her cell phone interrupted the tirade and instructions to Dee were reduced to hand signals and face pulling.

Bean and I exchanged glances. If this was showing Sophie style, no wonder Dee complained so much. It was worse than being in the army. Dolly, however, seemed to love her showing career—from what I could hear as she trotted around.

"Tra, la, la…oh, Crispin, you look in fine form today. Is that Bilbo Baggins? My word, he's put on weight, whatever are they feeding him? Yoo-hoo, Lady Macbeth, you look wonderful, darling. What is your human using on your coat? I can see my face in it!"

Sophie started up again: "Kick on, Dee, she's hardly moving. Get her going forward, she'll never catch the judge's eye like that! And *smile*, I said…"

"Jeez, Dee's mom's a total nightmare," I whispered to Bean. She raised her eyebrows and nodded dumbly.

James came flying back, having been to look at the overall scoreboard. Breathless, he skidded to a halt, colliding into Bean and knocking her flying.

"Sorry, Bean—but hey, guys, I've got news. With a fast clear from Katy and Bluey, we'll be in the top five teams."

"We haven't gone clear yet," said Katy, unraveling Bluey's tail bandage to reveal his braided tail. "And Bean's bound to do a fantastic test!" she added kindly.

Bean shook her head. "You know I'm going to forget the test," she replied. "But at least my score can be discounted now you've all done so well. I just wish I didn't have to go at all."

"We'll be disqualified if you don't, remember?" I reminded her.

"That's right," agreed James. "But with Katy and Bluey as our sure thing and guaranteed a clear round, we really have a chance!"

CHAPTER 18

IT WAS TIME FOR our sure things to do their stuff.

"Does anyone know how that cheating Dweeb pony did in the jumping?" asked Bean, holding Katy's off-side stirrup as Katy swung herself into Bluey's saddle.

"Shhh," said Katy, looking around to see if anyone had heard. "We can't say anything about that."

"She's last to jump," said James grimly.

"OK, guys," Katy said, patting Bluey's flecked neck. "Here we go. See you soon with good news, I hope."

Bluey was calmness personified as Drummer and Tiffany wished him luck.

"Go eat up those jumps, you machine!" said Tiffany.

"Nothing less than a fast clear is acceptable," Drummer yelled as a parting shot.

I gave Katy the thumbs-up sign. "Bluey's totally looking forward to it. No worries!" I told her.

Scott and Warrior were just finishing as we all got to the start of the cross-country. Warrior's breath came out in great puffs like a steam engine, and Scott looked cool, calm, and collected. Catriona and Leanne were there, too.

"Another clear round!" Cat said to us.

"Congratulations. Well done, Scott," James said.

"Yes, well done," I added.

"We don't cheat," Cat mouthed to me. I ignored my impulse to mouth back, "Oh, yes, you do!" We couldn't say anything about the Dweeb, and my conscience still bothered me. Was Cat right? Were we cheating? Was I cheating?

Katy and Bluey leaped over the first jump in a flash of purple and disappeared into the trees, out of sight. It would be some time before our teammates returned, but the commentator kept us up to speed. And they're clear over the second and going nicely to the third. A good leap over the ski jump, and onto the next jump where they're clear again." It was all going well so far. James was right—they were a sure thing.

"Come on, Bluey, do your stuff!" muttered Bean, her fingers crossed.

"Shhh, listen," I said. "They're announcing the results of Dee-Dee's class." The announcer from the showing rings boomed out over the loudspeaker.

"First, Datchets Dolly Daydream, ridden by Delia Wiseman, second…"

Whoever was second was drowned out by us all jumping up and down.

"*Yes!*" shouted James. "This is so our day. We're all going home with Brookdale ribbons. Yippee!"

"And she's qualified for HOYS," Bean pointed out.

"And the journey home with Sophie will be sweet. Imagine the atmosphere in the cab if Dee hadn't qualified!"

It didn't bear thinking about.

I suddenly became aware that the cross-country commentator was saying something I didn't want to hear. Something unbelievable.

"And they've jumped the wrong side of the flag—that's elimination."

"What's happened?" I cried. "They can't be talking about Katy, can they?"

The world seemed to stop as we all strained to hear the announcer. But we'd missed the drama, missed hearing exactly what had happened. Missed the moment it had all gone wrong for our sure things. Where did that leave the Great Eight?

Making our way to the finish, nobody dared to speak. I felt sick. Maybe we'd heard wrong, maybe the commentator had been mistaken. Bluey couldn't have gone wrong. Bluey never, ever went wrong.

Running back to the trailer, we got there just as Katy and Bluey arrived back, too.

"What happened?" demanded James.

Katy looked totally crestfallen—and near to tears.

"I'm so, so sorry, it was all my fault," she said, closing her eyes at the terrible memory as she jumped to the ground.

I could hear Bluey whispering, "Sorry, I couldn't help it. I just couldn't help it."

"It was the jump coming out of the woods," puffed Katy, tearing off her hat and running her fingers through her hair. "The sun was shining brightly, and after the darkness of the woods, neither of us could see where we were going. The sun was blinding—I could barely see. It's moved around the sky from where it was this morning when I walked the course."

"I saw the jump at the last moment," moaned Bluey, distraught at his mistake. "I thought I jumped it, but I was on the wrong side of the flag. I've let you all down."

"I messed up," continued Katy, unable to hear her pony. "The jump was narrow, it wasn't Bluey's fault. I couldn't believe it when I realized." She groaned, her shoulders sagging at the memory.

"Bluey's beside himself," I said, putting a supportive hand on Bluey's mane to show him we didn't blame him.

"Oh, Bluey, you couldn't help it," whispered Katy, kissing his cheek. "You're a star. You always will be."

"Yeah, Bluey, it's OK," said James.

"No one blames you," said Bean. But she looked white because with Katy and Bluey out of the competition, Bean's dressage score had to count. It was the only thing standing between the Great Eight's disgrace or glory.

Everybody knew it.

Nobody thought we stood a chance.

CHAPTER 19

KATY WAS DOING THE math—the trouble was, she was running out of fingers.

"We're not even in the running, now," she said, her eyes darting around the master scoreboard. "Because of me." She gulped.

"It was just one of those things, Katy. Don't dwell on it," said James.

"If India gets a fast clear with no time penalties, Team SLIC will beat us—we can't catch their score, even if Bean does remember her test," said Katy grimly.

"See, even you know I'm going to forget it!" wailed Bean. There was a long time to go before her event. Plenty of time for her nerves to turn to quaking terror.

"No, I don't, honest," mumbled Katy, fooling no one. So much for her confidence-boosting talk.

"But if India gets a fence down, or goes too slow," continued James, studying the scoreboard intently, "and if Bean gets a fabulous dressage score"—he winked at Bean, who stuck her tongue out at him—"the Great Eight could still finish high up in the placings, beating Team SLIC."

Beating Leanne's team mattered to me—simply because I had an old score to settle. The Dweeb shouldn't have been competing at all. It wasn't a level playing field. India—whether intentionally or not—wasn't eligible to even compete. Somehow, beating Team SLIC was what mattered most.

"OK, let's go and watch India's round," said James. "However painful it is, I need to see it with my own eyes."

"We'll have to be sporting and congratulate them." Katy sighed. "If they do beat us," she added, glancing at Bean. We all knew the chances of Bean getting a good dressage score were about a million to one. With Bluey's score discounted, our campaign was as good as over.

Why do we have to congratulate them? I thought. After all, they tried to get me disqualified. I didn't say anything out loud and remembered what my mom said about karma. But it was so hard, this karma thing! Katy was right, but knowing it didn't make it any easier. If we'd wanted to say something, we ought to have done so at the beginning, not now. We'd accepted the problem and run with it. It was too late to change our minds—that would just be spiteful. Bad karma.

We got to the show jumping ring just in time; India and the Dweeb were already halfway around the course, the Dweeb's careful hooves clearing the poles and planks with ease, concentration showing on her rider's face as India steered her talented pony over the beautiful jumps. The rest of her teammates stood in a huddle, willing her to a fast and clear round. I couldn't believe India knew about her pony's history. I just couldn't.

The Dweeb turned to the challenge of the final three jumps. They were nothing for an experienced pony, and India galloped through the finish with a neat, fast, clear round, to the joy of her team, who went wild. India's delight shone on her face as she pulled up outside the ring, surrounded by Cat, Scott, and Leanne, and her own mother, who had tears in her eyes.

"Oh, India, you were wonderful!" gushed her mother, dabbing her face with a tissue.

"No surprises there!" said James grimly.

But he was wrong.

Suddenly, the party was interrupted by a blond woman running up to the Dweeb. She patted her damp neck as she drew breath.

"Platinum Bell!" she shrieked so loudly, everyone around the ring could hear. "I won everything on this wonderful pony—at the Horse of the Year Show and here at Brookdale. It's wonderful to see her again!"

India smiled and shook her head, "I'm sorry, but this isn't…" she began.

India's mother froze. Then she grabbed the woman's arm and tried to pull her away.

"You're mistaken. This pony's not called Platinum Bell," she said almost too loudly, too quickly.

"Oh, I'd know her anywhere!" The blond woman laughed. "She's Bella all right—a bit older and her dapples have faded, but still the same. She was one of the most successful jumping ponies on the circuit!"

"What?" A woman with a formidable chest and a Jack Russell on a lead rope, whose son was on another team, joined in. "This pony's an experienced jumper, did you say?"

"Only one of the most successful ever!" The blond woman laughed.

"You don't know for sure," butted in India's mom. "You can't prove it."

"Well, she's still got the scar on her chest where she got caught up in the trailer one day," the woman said, pointing to a jagged black mark under the Dweeb's martingale strap.

We all looked at one another. The game was up. The color drained from India's face as the full force of the woman's words hit home.

"That pony shouldn't be here!" the chesty woman exclaimed, turning red with fury. Her son, on his dark bay cob, started whining that it wasn't fair, and the Jack Russell, sensing an upset, bounced about on the end of the leash, barking.

"You don't know what you're talking about!" replied India's mom, jutting her chin upward in defiance. But the large woman was having none of it.

"If that pony is who this woman says, she's too experienced for this competition. You're cheating, and I'm going to lodge an objection and get you disqualified."

India's mom went scarlet. It was clear that she'd known all along about the real identity of the Dweeb. I glanced at Team SLIC. They all stood with their mouths open, amazed. No one could doubt that it was a complete surprise to Scott, Cat, and poor India—although James had told Leanne, she was still horrified at the scene in front of her.

The crowd started whispering in excitement as the woman marched off on her mission to get India disqualified.

"Is this true, Mom?" India whispered.

"Well, India, I, er, I didn't know anything about this, honestly," her mom stammered. It was obvious she was lying.

"Oh, Mom, how could you?" cried India, bursting into tears.

"Look, sweetie, I just wanted you to do well. I just wanted success for you, for you to be happy. I wanted you to win. I did it for you…"

"God, this is just awful," I heard Bean whisper. "Poor India."

I felt sorry for her, too. It wasn't her fault. It didn't seem fair somehow.

"So you cheated!" yelled India. "And you made me cheat, too."

India's mom flinched like she'd been hit.

"And you made me let all my teammates down!" India continued, turning toward Team SLIC, who stood there silent and shocked, seeing all their hard work and dreams sliding away.

"But I did it because I love you, India, don't you understand?" her mom pleaded.

"That's too bad, because I hate you for it!" sobbed India, turning the Dweeb and cantering off across the showground.

For the second time that day I was grateful for my own parents. They're weird, but they'd never do anything like India's mom. She must have totally blown it with the karma thing. I thought I'd feel glad if India was found out, but instead, I couldn't help feeling sorry for the disappointment the whole team was experiencing. In her effort to see her daughter succeed, India's mother had ruined any chance of success for the whole team. It was totally unfair, and our rivals didn't deserve it. I couldn't imagine how poor India must have been feeling right now. I didn't feel any better when Team SLIC's marks got wiped from the scoreboard. We'd been upset about them cheating, but when they were actually eliminated, we didn't feel victorious at all.

And then another, heart-stopping thought hit me: Now that Cat was out of the competition, would she resurrect her campaign to get the Great Eight disqualified, too? Would she come gunning for me?

Chapter 20

"ARE YOU OK, BEAN?" asked Katy, as we all walked back to base. Bean nodded, robot-like. She looked ashen and anything but OK. We helped her get Tiffany ready. Actually, we got Tiffany ready—Bean couldn't do anything, she was in such a state. If Bean didn't compete, we'd be disqualified, and nobody wanted that. We'd come this far, we wanted desperately to finish. All the teams would parade in the main ring, and we didn't want to go home robbed of that chance. Like Team SLIC had been, I couldn't help thinking.

Dee braided Bean's hair and Sophie—all smiles now that Dolly and Dee had qualified for HOYS—sprayed Tiffany with Dolly's very expensive show sheen, making her golden coat glimmer.

"With any luck, the judges will be so dazzled by Tiff's gleaming coat, they won't notice they're not actually doing the test," Sophie whispered.

As we walked over to the dressage arena, Bean's face turned even paler. Anxiously, I glanced at James and Katy who were keeping uncharacteristically quiet. They had to be sharing my negative feelings—and the India incident had left everyone feeling a bit wobbly. Swinging from Katy's hand like an instrument of torture was the noseband, ready to encase Tiff at the last moment. It seemed like the final insult—wearing a noseband for ritual humiliation in a test Bean couldn't remember.

"I'm going to let you all down," Bean whispered shakily.

"No, you're not, Bean," I said, my heart pounding. I hoped my face didn't show my fears. "Just do your best. No one's expecting any more than that."

Bean bit her lip and stayed silent in terror.

"You just have to do as much as you can remember, we don't want to be disqualified," said James, aiming a plastic smile at Bean.

If Bean was despondent, Tiffany was in a determined mood. I could hear her muttering to herself under her breath. "You can do this, Tiff, noseband or no noseband. Come on, girl! This is the final time, and you can do it, you can, you can—"

"It's time," James declared. Bean looked at him like a condemned prisoner about to have her head cut off.

Katy fumbled with the noseband, but this time, Tiffany didn't close her eyes. She took a deep breath, and as their names were announced, the palomino trotted into the ring and around the outside of the dressage markers, waiting for the bell. I sidled up to James.

"Do you think Cat will try to get me disqualified again, too?" I asked him.

James's grinned. "There wouldn't be much point now," he said grimly. "It's not like we've got a chance, is there?"

"But she still might," I said, chewing my nails. I didn't think Cat was the charitable sort.

The bell sounded and, miserably, we all leaned on the rails. Would Bean remember the test? Even if she did, she couldn't possibly get a good enough score to make up for Katy and Bluey's shock elimination. Bean and Tiffany entered at C and rode straight up the centerline—but something was already wrong. Bean started to look wildly about her, as though she'd just woken up and hadn't a clue where she was.

"Oh, no," wailed Katy, "she doesn't know where to go next."

"It's going to be a disaster," Dee said, her fist in her mouth.

"Come on, Bean," whispered James, gripping the rails. "Come on."

But Bean sat like a dummy giving no signals to Tiffany, offering no suggestions of where to go.

Even though I had known, deep in my heart, that any chance the Great Eight had of doing well disappeared when Katy and Bluey jumped to the wrong side of the flag, I had still allowed myself to believe that Bean might, against all the odds, remember this all-important, rehearsed-a-million-times test.

Just this one test.

Just this once.

But now I knew I'd been kidding myself.

"She's forgotten the test!" I breathed. "She said she would, and we didn't believe her. It's the end of the Great Eight's bid for glory!"

CHAPTER 21

THE WHOLE WORLD SEEMED to slow down. Bean looked around frantically, obviously unable to remember where to go and what to do. Disqualification stared the Great Eight squarely in the face.

"Oh, I can't look!" breathed Katy, her head in her hands.

"We should never have made her do the dressage." James sighed—conveniently forgetting that he had been the one who'd had insisted on it.

"She told us she'd forget!" I muttered. "She told us all along!"

"Hold on…" Dee said, grabbing my sleeve. "Look!"

We all watched, breathless and openmouthed as something amazing happened. Instead of disaster, Bean and Tiffany began their test. Tiffany pranced around the corner in perfect rhythm, and Bean suddenly sat up, quiet and still, looking more like a dressage rider with every step. They progressed with Tiffany on the bit, her paces even and with no sign of resistance, looking as though they competed in dressage every day of their lives.

"I told her she could do it!" said James, letting his breath out with a *whoosh*.

"She's fantastic!" whispered Katy, scared to say it any louder.

Even wearing the hateful noseband, Tiffany was doing a great job, and Bean was like a rider possessed. It looked wonderful—Bean's blond braid matching her pony's golden coat exactly, bouncing gently on the back of her navy jacket. Their transitions were right on the letters, their turns and circles flowing and balanced, and their paces regular. Tiffany didn't shake her head once. As they finished, we all let out a whoop of delight. It had been a fantastic test. In fact, I thought, it was as though Bean had been replaced by a Bean look-alike who was fabulous at dressage. It was uncanny!

By the time we got to her outside the ring, the noseband lay in the grass, and Bean was hugging her pony, tears streaming down her face.

"Tiffany, you're amazing!" she kept saying, hugging Tiffany again and again.

"*You* were amazing!" shouted Dee.

"Bean, that was fantastic!" I said.

"Wow, Bean, you've been holding out on us. That was the best test ever!" cried James, shaking his head in disbelief.

"Way to go, Bean!" shouted Katy. "We told you you'd remember the test!"

"But I didn't," said Bean.

"You so did!" I yelled.

"No, it wasn't me. My mind went to mush as soon as I entered the arena," Bean said, wiping her eyes on her sleeves. "I just sat there, in a trace."

"But we saw you…" began Dee.

"It was Tiffany," explained Bean, hugging her pony again. "She did it all. She remembered the whole test. Thank goodness we practiced it at home."

We all turned to Tiff, speechless.

"I promised I'd do my best," I heard Tiffany whisper.

"But it didn't look like Tiff was doing it at all," said Katy, astounded. "I mean, all the transitions were perfect and everything."

"I know where to do it. Give me some credit." Tiffany snorted. I told the others. We just couldn't believe it.

"That's got to be a good score," said James. He was all excited, looking toward the scoreboard.

"Oh, here comes the score now! I can't look!" muttered Katy as one of the Sublime Equine girls wrote Bean and Tiffany's score on the board.

"How much?" Bean gasped in disbelief.

We all stared at the board.

"Seventy-three!" yelled Katy, jumping up in the air and letting out a whoop of delight. "You're so the dressage queen, Bean!"

"Bean, Bean, dressage queen," chanted Dee, thumping Bean on the back.

"Look out, Leanne, there's a new kid on the block!" said Katy.

"Oh, Tiff, you are clever," Bean whispered to her pony, swinging off her neck in a bear hug.

"Careful," I heard Tiffany say. "I think that's a life-threatening object over there...and there's a funny noise around here…and I never *ever* want to wear that awful noseband again!"

And then I heard another voice I'd been dreading. It was anything but happy.

"You are so a cheat, Pia. I'm going to see that your team is disqualified."

Catriona!

"Oh, Cat, don't be like that," said James in a soothing voice. "Getting us disqualified won't help your team."

"Please, Cat," said Bean, aghast. "How could you? We've always been friends, haven't we?"

"You wouldn't be so mean, surely?" added Katy.

"I don't see why you should be in this competition when we've been disqualified. You're cheating worse than us, with Pia here being able to communicate with her pony in the wild card event," Cat said nastily.

"But you never believed I could talk to ponies!" I said.

"Yeah, well, it's not what I believe, is it? It's what the organizers believe!"

"Even if Pia can talk to the ponies," said Katy carefully, "she can't make them perform any better, can she? You're being unreasonable, Cat."

"Come on, Cat," added James, winking at her. "Be a sport!"

Cat's green eyes looked at James. "It isn't fair," she said. "You know it isn't. Why should she get away with it? Maybe you shouldn't have had her on your team!" With that, Cat turned around and marched off in the direction of the secretary's tent.

"How can she be so vindictive?" asked Katy. Our euphoria had been short-lived. Now we were all plunged back into despair.

"She's not just hurting Pia, she's hurting all of us," said Bean. "We all used to be such good friends. I don't know why she's being so nasty."

Katy gave Bean a bit of a look. "It's not just because of India," she said. "She's upset because...oh, you know."

Bean nodded. "That's not our fault." She sighed. "She's taking it out on us."

"What are you not telling me?" I said, desperate to know the secret everyone but me seemed to know about Catriona. No one answered.

"I'm going to talk to her..." said James, turning around and heading off after Cat. "See you back at the trailer."

"What do you think he's going to do?" asked Dee.

"Kill her?" suggested Bean.

"If anyone can persuade Cat, James can," Katy said thoughtfully.

I wondered what she could possibly mean. Could James save the Great Eight a second time? I felt terrible. Everyone at the yard had been friends before I arrived. My pony whispering had altered things. It was because of me Bean was saying she would never see Cat in the same light again. Because of me Katy said she would never have thought Cat capable of being so mean. Because of me James was going...to do what? Was Cat right? Was I cheating? I decided karma sucked.

Back at the horse trailer, we waited around miserably for James to return. I didn't see how he could stop Cat from lodging an objection. Around us, the show went on—horses left the trailer park for their events, ponies returned with riders who were either euphoric or downcast, grooms rode in their charges.

Suddenly, James was back, breathless and red in the face from running.

"Get saddled up!" he shouted. "We're due in the ring any time now!"

"What?" We all gaped at him, unable to take in the significance of his words.

"Come on—we're still in the competition, and they're due to announce the winners at any moment!"

A wave of relief washed over me. James had done it—I didn't care how. Hastily, we bridled the ponies, and Dee helped me into her showing outfit—I'd forgotten my jacket and hat, only packing my wild card getup.

"But what about Cat?" asked Katy.

"It's all sorted out," James said dismissively, vaulting into Moth's saddle and cantering off in the direction of the main ring.

"Who cares about the whys and hows?!" shouted Katy. "Let's go!"

Having abandoned the scoreboard in despair when Cat had appeared, we had no idea where the Great Eight were placed. All the teams milled around the entrance to the main ring and the Sublime Equine promo girls were putting the teams in order as the commentator was telling the crowd about the Sublime Equine bigwigs who were presenting the prizes. The managing director of Sublime Equine, a woman in a lime-green suit and an expensive-looking hairdo, struggled onto the grass with a huge trophy.

"First place in the Sublime Equine Challenge goes to..." boomed the voice on the loudspeaker.

We knew it wasn't us. We'd worked that much out at the scoreboard.

"Team Stapleford Stables!"

Stapleford Stables were so good. Three members of their team had won their events—pretty impressive and impossible to beat. They rode into the arena to thunderous applause.

"Which team are you?" asked a Sublime Equine promo girl.

"The Great Eight," Katy replied. "Have we placed anywhere?"

The girl examined her clipboard. "Don't you know? Er, let me see. The Great Eight...can't see you on here..."

That doesn't sound promising, I thought with a sinking heart.

The loudspeaker drowned out the promo girl. "Second place goes to the Great Eight, James Beecham on Gypsy Moth, Charlotte Beanie on Tiffany...."

The whole world seemed to stop. I looked at my fellow teammates, and they looked back at me. I don't think any one of us had our mouths closed.

"Come on, hurry up!" said the Sublime Equine promo girl, shooing us along the famous Brookdale tunnel I'd seen on TV and into the ring.

Riding Drummer in the famous arena, flanked by James and Moth, Bean and Tiffany, and Katy and Bluey, I knew what it felt like to win an Olympic medal—I couldn't have felt happier or more proud of our team. Everyone cheered and clapped. We heard our names over the loudspeaker, and I thought this was the most amazing moment of my whole life. Drummer took it all in stride, of course, but Bluey felt like me. I could hear him being all proud and excited. We had to box Tiffany in because of all the jumps, and officials and photographers were making her freak. Moth was her usual, silent, trembly self.

We weren't. We hugged one another, and pointed out people in the crowd—I could see Dad and Skinny Lynny actually in the tunnel (so I supposed wearing jodhpurs had its advantages—the organizers had obviously mistaken Lyn for a competitor!).

The ribbons were huge! We got two each—a second prize one, and an orange and lime finalist one. With one on either side of his bridle, I could hear Drum complaining that he felt like a blinkered cart horse.

But that wasn't all. After the team prize giving (and we all won finalist certificates for Sublime Equine outfits, as well as one hundred dollars in cash each!), the announcer called out the winners of each individual event. I wasn't really listening—I was busy looking around to see if I could

169

spot Mom in the crowd—so when James gave me a shove, I was just about to shove him back when I felt everyone looking in my direction. Something, it seemed, was expected of me.

"That's you!" hissed James.

"What is?" I said, being stupid.

"You've won the wild card event!" shouted Bean.

"You and Drum have prevented Team Stapleford Stables from cleaning up in every event!" James told me.

"Go on! Go and get your prize!" said Katy.

I steered Drummer forward so that the managing director of Sublime Equine could present me with another huge ribbon, a trophy, and another check for one hundred dollars. I couldn't believe it—especially when they got to the best bit, a fabulous blue Brookdale sash, which was like the Holy Grail to me. My face hurt, I was grinning so much.

When we all galloped around the vast arena on our lap of honor with the crowd's applause ringing in our ears, it was a moment I knew I'd remember for the rest of my life. And when Drummer kicked out a huge buck, I laughed and patted him in thanks for a job well done. My pony was such a star, and I was determined that he'd never feel unappreciated again. The Sublime Equine Challenge had been the most fantastic fun—but the fact that we'd learned more about our relationships with our ponies was worth more than the huge ribbons, more than the prize money, even my coveted sash—although they were fabulous, too!

It was a fairy-tale ending to our challenge—perhaps karma had worked for us after all.

Somewhere in the back of my mind was the niggling question of how James had persuaded Cat not to lodge an objection against me. I couldn't imagine what he could have said to stop her, but right then I didn't care. Whatever he'd said, it was worth it, I thought. No one could take away this fabulous feeling I was experiencing in the Brookdale main arena. I just wished I could have put out of my mind the image of poor India when she realized her dream had ended through no fault of her own, and the toe-curling feeling that the rift between me and Cat had gone beyond any point of repair.

CHAPTER 22

THANKS, DRUM, I LOVE you so much," I whispered into one of Drum's furry, black-tipped ears as we stood in the field at home.

"Mmmm." Drummer snorted, his black mane still curled and fluffy from the braids. "I think I've had enough appreciation for one day. It's been death-by-hugging ever since we got those huge, poofy blobs that pass for ribbons slapped on either side of me. I felt claustrophobic!"

"Oh, you loved it really!" I said, hugging him again. "And it's all over now."

"Does that mean I'll be treated with a bit more respect? I mean"—he glared at me—"no more bells?"

I laughed. "OK, no more bells. I promise!"

Drum sank to his knees, sighing with the effort of rolling right over and getting both sides good and dusty. Rising with a grunt, a shake began at his head, rippling all the way through his body to his tail, the dust wafting off him in a cloud. I watched as he wandered over to the water trough for a long drink before settling down with the others in an all-night grass-munching session. I had the best pony in the whole world—bar none.

Unpinning Epona from my pocket, I took her out and looked at her, rubbing the spot where her nose used to be.

"Thanks for your help, Epona," I whispered. Without her, I would never be able to hear Drum and the other ponies. She was worth all the trouble that always seemed to come with her.

Back at the yard, Bean was showing Mrs. Collins her ribbons, Katy was mucking out her stable, and James was lolling around on a bench outside the tack room, stroking Swish. He seemed a bit quiet after all the highs and lows of the day.

"I suppose that's the end of the Great Eight," declared Katy, throwing dirty straw into the wheelbarrow.

"We were pretty great, after all!" mused James.

"The ponies were," I corrected him.

"Oh, yes, the ponies were just amazing!" agreed Bean, locking her tack box. "Especially mine!"

Mrs. Collins flip-flopped back to the house in her slippers, scooping up Twiddles-scissor-paws with her on the way.

"We have to take some of the credit, though," said Katy, shoving her fork into the barrow and pushing it out of her stable. "I mean, we overcame our problems and our doubts, and we did wonderfully."

"You mean you bullied us into it!" Bean reminded her.

"Yes, Katy, you'd make an awesome sports coach." James yawned.

"That's right, Katy, you have to take some credit, too," I said. The sight of James yawning had made me suddenly very tired. We'd been up for hours and hours, and now the excitement had died down, I suddenly felt like I could sleep

173

for a week. I felt deliriously happy and content—this was definitely going in my diary as one of my best-ever days. I couldn't wait to display my Brookdale sash in my bedroom, next to Drummer's ribbons. I still couldn't believe we'd won it. There was just one thing that had spoiled everyone's day.

"I still don't get it about the Dweeb," mused Bean.

I saw James roll his eyes. Unfortunately, so did Bean.

"Don't do that, James. How did India's mom pass Platinum Bell off for the Dweeb? We all had to show our ponies' passports at Brookdale."

"She's right," said Katy.

I shrugged. "She must have forged the passport."

"Or Platinum Bell was passed off as another pony by India's mom before passports came into force," suggested James. "She's not exactly young."

"What's India's mom's age got to do with it?" asked Bean.

"No, Platinum Bell's not exactly young," I explained.

"Of course!" said Katy. "I bet India's mom wasn't the first person to profit from the deception—although she obviously knew about it."

"I still don't understand it," I said. "I know she wanted India to win, but what a dreadful way to do it! And do you know what?"

"What?" said Bean.

"I know it was unfair of Platinum Bell to be in the competition, but somehow it still feels unfair that poor India was disqualified—along with her whole team. I mean, she didn't know."

"I know what you mean," agreed Katy. "I wanted to beat Team SLIC fair and square, not have them taken out of the competition. It's awkward."

"And it's going to get worse, seeing Leanne and Cat here every day," Bean pointed out.

"That's true," James agreed, stroking Swish behind his ear. Swish's hind leg thumped the ground—James obviously knew the exact spot to tickle.

"I still want to know what you said to Cat, James," said Katy.

"Don't ask." James groaned. "She was really upset—the whole team was crushed. You can't blame them."

"So what did you say to her?" asked Katy. She wasn't going to let it go.

"I just asked her," said James.

"Well, we asked her. She didn't do it for us," said Bean.

James shrugged. He seemed suddenly very interested in Swish's collar. "I just asked her," he repeated quietly.

Suddenly, I didn't want to know how James had persuaded Cat.

"You asked her out!" Katy exploded, the words piercing my heart. "You know Cat likes you!" Katy went on, her words digging deeper and deeper into my soul. "You did a deal!"

Bean stood openmouthed, looking from Katy to James. There was no doubt that Katy had guessed the truth. James didn't deny it.

Because of me James was going out with Catriona.

Because of me…

"Shhh!" hissed James as Dee returned from turning Dolly out for the night.

"I told you, didn't I?" Dee said, oblivious to the atmosphere on the yard.

"Told us what?" said James quickly, obviously relieved at the change of subject.

"I told you Granddad would help us. And he did!"

"Are you serious?" said Bean, astonished.

"Yeah, good old Granddad. I knew he'd come through. You have him to thank for your Brookdale success! Oh, and me, of course!"

Four of the Great Eight exchanged glances.

"Get her!" yelled James, leaping up and grabbing Dee, pinning her arms to her sides.

"Get off me!" Dee shrieked, kicking out as James lifted her clean off the ground.

Katy grabbed one leg, Bean the other, and I helped James at the heavy end as we carried Dee, kicking and screaming, to the field.

"Whatever are you doing?" shouted Sophie, looking over Lester's half door. Lester's liver chestnut ears were twitching at the racket, and he backed into his stable, snorting.

"Just going to dump her in the trough!" said James, without breaking pace, like it was the most natural thing in the world.

"Oh," said Sophie. "Do it quickly, will you? You're upsetting Lester."

Dee's mom is so weird, you just never know which way she's going to go.

"*No!*" screamed Dee. "I'm warning you, don't you dare, *dare*, put me in the trough…Mom…*help!*"

"We'll teach you," muttered James.

"Yes, Dee, give the ponies some credit!" demanded Katy.

"And us!" added Bean, grimly hanging on to Dee's thrashing right leg.

"We," I said as we dropped Dee into the water, "are the Great Eight! And don't you forget it!"

Dee gasped as she hit the cold water, and she thrashed about, making herself even wetter. "I'm so going to get you all for this!" she spluttered furiously.

The ponies all lifted their heads and stared—except Tiffany: she took off down the field at a gallop, giving us a view of her tail.

"Oh, that's nice," said Drummer. "How would you like us to come and dunk ourselves in your drinking water?"

"We'll clean it out," I assured him, a mass of emotions whirling around my head and my heart.

Because of me, Cat was James's girlfriend.

It seemed that Cat had her own victory after all.

COMING SOON...

The Pony Whisperer

SECRET PONY SOCIETY

I HAD HOPED THAT A carefree Saturday morning ride would push my latest problem to the back of my mind for a while. And in a way, it turned out like that because by the time Drummer and I got back, I had a whole new bunch of things to worry about. "It's so lush here," he wailed, looking around at all the emerald blades waving in the breeze by the side of the newly ploughed field, "and it's just going to waste." I pretended I couldn't hear him. If I could keep it up, he might think I'd left Epona behind. He knows that without her I'm just like everybody else; I can't hear an equine word.

"It will be winter soon," he went on, "and there'll be no good grass left. Everyone knows you should let ponies build up fat reserves for the coming lean months. I'm surprised you don't know that. You think you know lots about pony management. Obviously, you don't know as much as you think."

He was trying to rile me, and it was starting to work. My bright bay pony knows exactly which of my buttons to push to get a reaction. I squeezed his sides, and Drum broke into a trot with a theatrical sigh about leaving the grass. I wouldn't mind, but he's already bordering on the tubby side.

Since I'd gone back to school after summer vacation, my riding had been limited to weekends and evenings. With the days getting shorter, evening riding meant everyone jostling for space in the floodlit outdoor school, so that Saturday, it was great to ride in open spaces for a change. We cantered around the field then turned into the woods, Drummer's hoofbeats silent on the moss. Red and golden leaves fluttered unhurriedly to the ground, and there was a damp autumn smell heralding bleak days to come.

And that's when the first odd thing occurred.

Suddenly, Drummer froze to a halt, shooting me forward. Luckily, as he did so, his head shot right up like a giraffe's, keeping me in the saddle. Following the direction of his ears I could see his gaze fixed on something moving through the trees, and I squinted in the same direction, expecting to see a deer. The woods are riddled with them, and Drummer always overreacts. You'd think they were stegosauruses or something.

It wasn't a deer (or a stegosaurus). It was a pony. An unfamiliar, dark gray—almost black—pony, its black mane and tail laced with white highlights that glinted silver in shafts of sunlight twinkling through the branches. Catching my breath, I watched as it moved through the trees.

The pony wasn't alone. A girl sat astride the bare, black back. She wore no hat and her long, black hair fanned out behind her as her pony cantered and hopped over fallen branches, the pair fused together as though glued. And then I noticed the dog running alongside; a large, leggy hound, like a squire to a knight, keeping his nose level with the girl's toes, matching the pony stride for stride.

I felt the hairs on the back of my neck stand up as the trio disappeared in the gloom. Involuntarily, I shivered. Then I realized that I wasn't the only one holding my breath.

"That's spooky!" exclaimed Drummer, his breath coming out in a *whooh,* my legs rising against his sides as he exhaled.

"You don't think..." I trailed off, reluctant to put my thoughts into words. The trio had been so strange and had moved so silently. I so didn't want to use the word *ghost.*

The whole area around Laurel Farm stables, the stable where I keep Drummer, is rich in history and atmosphere. Since Roman times it had been the location of settlements and mansions, taking advantage of the high ground. Drummer's stable yard used to be a farm for a huge country house that no longer exists. It was that history that had given me Epona and changed my life.

I couldn't help thinking that the mysterious rider and her pony and dog certainly looked as though they belonged to a bygone age. I mean, whoever nowadays goes riding without a hat?

"They wouldn't be the first spirits I've seen around here," mumbled Drummer, snorting. My heart missed a beat, and my thoughts flew back to the séance we'd held at the stables in the summer. Dee had insisted on trying to call up her dead granddad to help us with a team riding competition. The séance had scared us all out of our minds, and I didn't welcome the reminder now, in the gloom of the trees. The woods suddenly seemed very spooky and the very place *not* to be, especially with the wind whispering through the trees.

"What else have you seen?" I asked Drum, winding my fingers through his mane for comfort, half hoping he wouldn't tell me.

"So you can hear me, then?" asked Drum, turning and giving me a look with his big, brown left eye. "Pretend you can't hear me when grass is the subject, but you're all ears when there's something you want to talk about!"

"Oh, you're impossible!" I said angrily. "You are not supposed to eat when we're on a ride, you know that. It's really bad manners, and you'll get green gunk on your bit."

"*Oooooo-eee-oooo,*" said Drum. I couldn't tell whether he was being snarky, or whether he was making ghost noises. Either way, it wasn't funny.

At least the strange girl and her pony were a distraction from my own doom and gloom—momentarily, anyway. Things had taken a downward turn at the stable recently, and I didn't want to think about that. The trouble was, the more I tried to blot it out of my mind, the more it insisted on creeping back in. Actually, it tended to gallop in rather than creep. It occupied my mind like an invading army, sweeping all good events and thoughts before it and enforcing its dominant, depressing regime at full power.

I made Drummer canter along a path in the woods

that we call the Winding Canter (for obvious reasons) and at the end, we burst out of the darkness of the trees and back into the weak autumn sunshine at the top of the hill. Then, without a breather (so Drum couldn't nag me), we walked briskly down the hill to the lane, intending to cross it and continue on the bridle path in a big circle around Clanmore Common, before returning home.

I couldn't stop thinking about the mysterious girl and her pony. That the pony was well-bred had been obvious, with its fine legs and neat head. The girl had been slim and had sat easily like an expert rider, her legs relaxed and dangling next to her pony's sides. Wherever had she come from? Laurel Farm wasn't the only stable in the area—there were plenty of stables and farmers who rented fields to the local horsey population. And if she wasn't a ghost and if I could get near enough, I might be able to learn more about them—if I could hear what the pony was saying, anyway. At least, I could with Epona in my pocket.

Epona, I had discovered, had been a goddess of horses, worshipped by the ancient Celts and Romans. Ever since I'd stumbled (well, Drummer had done the stumbling, actually) across the tiny stone statue of a woman—Epona—seated sidesaddle on a horse, I'd been able to hear what horses and ponies were saying—for better or worse—whenever I had her with me. I never leave home without her now. To say Epona has changed my life is putting it mildly—I'm known as the Pony Whisperer, for a start, as I can hear and talk to horses and ponies. You'd think that would be fantastic, wouldn't you? But it has its downsides—and was the cause of my latest worry that I had come out to forget.

Halfway down the hill, as we got near to the lane, something happened that did manage to distract me and put my own worries very firmly into perspective. With a droning noise, two huge four-by-four vehicles drove along the tarmac, dangerously straddling both lanes, their lights flashing as they drove past and into the distance. Birds suddenly flew out of the bushes and trees, and a soft hum and clattering from the cars' wake got louder and louder. Familiar sounds of horses' hooves mingled with shouting and revved car engines and, instinctively, Drum and I drew back among the trees, looking down from our natural vantage point toward the approaching commotion. The hoofbeats got louder, the shouts more urgent, more intense, and we waited to see what would come around the bend.

I expected to see horses, but when three came into view, turning the corner abreast and thundering toward us, my feelings of excitement turned to dread.

ABOUT THE AUTHOR

Janet Rising's work with horses has included working at a donkey stud, producing show ponies, and teaching both adults and children, with a special interest in helping nervous riders enjoy their sport, as well as training owners on how to handle their horses and ponies from the ground. Always passionate about writing, Janet's first short story was published when she was fourteen, and for the past ten years she has been editor of *PONY,* Britain's top-selling horsey teen magazine.